Work.
Rest.
Repeat.

by
Frank Tayell

Dedicated to family and friends

Copyright 2014
All rights reserved
All people, places and events are fictional.

The author has asserted their moral right under the Copyright, Designs and Patents Act, 1988, to be identified as the author of this work. All rights reserved. No part of this publication may be reproduced, copied, stored in a retrieval system, or transmitted, in any form or by any means, without the prior written consent of the copyright holder, nor be otherwise circulated in any form of binding or cover other than that in which it is published and without a similar condition being imposed on the subsequent purchaser.

ISBN-13: 978-1502356161
ISBN-10: 1502356163

Other titles:
Surviving The Evacuation
Book 0.5: Zombies vs The Living Dead
Book 1: London
Book 2: Wasteland
Book 3: Family
&
Undead Britain
(A short story in the anthology; 'At Hell's Gate')

For information on old, new and upcoming releases, please visit
www.FrankTayell.com
www.facebook.com/FrankTayell
twitter.com/FrankTayell

Prologue - An Ordinary Shift
Twenty-six hours before voting begins

Ely ducked. The fist sailed past his face. As he straightened something struck the side of his head. His helmet took the brunt of the impact, but he staggered forwards, knocking two of the brawling workers to the floor.

Half turning, he lashed out and grabbed a fistful of cloth and arm. He didn't know if it was the person who'd struck him. He didn't care. He threw the felon to the ground as his other hand scrabbled for the truncheon on his belt. When he pulled it out he found the grip unfamiliar. He'd not used the baton for years, not even in practice. Another blow struck him, this time to the back of his neck. The truncheon fell from his fingers and was forgotten as his helmet was dislodged. His display pixelated as it tried to reset. He was blind.

He roared with anger, tore the helmet off and began swinging it left and right. With his other hand he grabbed and pulled the brawling workers apart.

Someone screamed in pain. He didn't see whom, but the noise reminded Ely that he was the Constable of Tower-One. He was responsible for maintaining law and order. He was responsible for keeping the workers safe.

"Stop!" he yelled, turning his incoherent roar into a barked command. "Stop! I order you to stop!"

Cowed more by his berserker thrashing than by his words, the fight broke up and the workers moved apart.

"Stop." This time the word came out more quietly. Ely was breathing hard. He'd finished his fourteen hours on duty and had been halfway through his six hours of Recreation when he'd received the alert.

"No! No one move. Don't even think about it, unless you want me to charge you with fleeing a crime scene as well." He addressed this to those edging towards the doors at the back of the crowd. It wouldn't matter if they did try to creep away. The cameras would have recorded their actions, the chips in their wristboard computers logging their presence in the room at the time of the fight. There was no hiding from guilt, no escaping justice.

The crowd stopped moving and, one by one, turned their collective eyes on the three people lying prostrate on the floor.

Ely cursed as he looked down. One of them seemed... not too serious. The man was rolling from side to side clutching his arm, his eyes tightly shut, his teeth gritted against the pain. A break, Ely guessed. Probably just a fracture. The man was bleeding, but only from a shallow cut on his forehead. No, it was nothing serious, nothing that couldn't be treated in the infirmary up on Level Seventy-Seven. It was the other two who'd captured the attention of the crowd. Neither was moving.

Ely put his helmet back on. It took a moment for the retinal scan to log him back into the Tower's surveillance system. He pulled up the camera feeds for the privacy rooms around the lounge's perimeter to check that no one was lurking within. They were all empty.

A moment after that, two alerts came up on his display, one for each of the two prone men. Their vital signs, monitored by the wristboard computers, were shallow.

As per procedure Ely checked to see if the infirmary had been automatically alerted. It had. The two nurses were already on their way down, yet Ely could tell that the two unconscious felons would require more expert treatment. They would have to be transported to the hospital in Tower-Thirteen.

He cursed again, but feeling that his duty of care had been fulfilled he turned to look at the mob. As he moved his gaze from worker to worker, a tag appeared on his display, giving their names and criminal probability. For each of them, that number was set at one hundred percent.

"Do you know what you've done?" he asked the crowd. "Look at them. Do you know what this means?"

No one spoke. Some looked shocked, others ashamed.

"You know that when they recover they won't be coming back here," Ely said. "They'll be re-assigned to one of the other Towers. Where will that leave our production targets?"

The City of Britain consisted of thirteen Towers jutting up out of the rising sea. Each was home to around twelve thousand citizens. Tower-Thirteen contained the hospital, the large retirement home, the prison, the advanced training school, and the administrative hub for the City. Towers Two through Twelve were the Factories where the components for the colony ships were made. Tower-One housed the Assemblies, where each of those components was checked and rechecked before being transported to the launch site. There, the first three colony ships were in the final stages of construction.

Work in the Assemblies of Tower-One was hard, but unlike labouring in the Factory-Towers, it wasn't dangerous. Not a shift went by without the newsfeeds reporting a serious, or sometimes fatal, injury from one of them. On leaving the hospital workers from Tower-One, and those felons who'd completed their sentence working on one of the penal gangs at the launch site, were always re-allocated to one of the Factories. In terms of Tower-One's productivity, being sent to the hospital was as good as being dead.

"It's one year until the first ship will be ready to launch," Ely growled at the mob. "One year! The ballot will be held next week, and you all jeopardise your chance of winning a place on it by brawling like... like..." He couldn't think of a word that appropriately expressed his disgust.

A sudden, terrible, thought struck him.

"No one move," he snapped unnecessarily as he pulled up the footage from the fight onto his display. He quickly cycled through the recordings from the different cameras, switching between the ones affixed to the ceilings and doors, the ones worn on the visors of the individual workers, and the one in his own helmet. He relaxed. All the people he'd hit were still standing.

"Control," Ely spoke into the ever-open microphone on his collar.

"Constable?" The soft voice of Vauxhall, Tower-One's Controller, came clearly through his earpiece.

"I need to report an affray. Lounge-Two." Except it wasn't called that anymore. "The uh... Sailor's Rest," he corrected himself. "It's under control, but at least two workers will require hospitalisation." There was a shuffling of feet. He raised his voice. "Inform the council."

"Of course," the Controller said. "But if they're awake they'll already have received the alert sent to the infirmary."

That was true enough, and they would all be awake. The election was just over three shifts away. It was a foregone conclusion that Councillor Cornwall would be elected Chancellor by a landslide.

"Do any of you wish to admit your guilt?" Ely asked the crowd. He doubted anyone would. They never did. It didn't matter. He had the camera footage. Up until the Re-Organisation four years ago there had been the audio-feed as well. Then the right to privacy had been amended to the City of Britain's Constitution, and Ely's job got more time consuming, though not more difficult. Other than maintaining a watch against sedition, sabotage and recidivism, the only crimes the Constable usually dealt with were the occasional fights. This one was more serious than any he had dealt with before, but he saw no difficulties in resolving it.

He turned his attention back to the images projected onto the inside of his visor. The system had already finished a preliminary analysis of the footage from the past thirty minutes. It had tagged each occasion when a citizen had hit, collided, pushed or in any other way interacted with another worker.

One of the unconscious men twitched violently. Ely ignored the distraction, as he went through the footage, identifying which of those occasions constituted an offence.

Most of the crowd had launched a kick or thrown a punch, but there were seven people who'd done more. Leaving the two unconscious men and the third man still whimpering in pain aside, he focused his attention on the other four.

Juliana Dundee had thrown the blow that had dented his helmet, but it was clear she'd done it accidentally whilst trying to escape the melee in the centre of the room.

The other two, Ashford and Leeds, had initially acted in self-defence, then kept going when instinct overtook reason. He docked them forty points each. That left the other four.

Edmund Lundy, one of the two men on the floor, had thrown the first punch at Gerald Carlisle. *Mr* Gerald Carlisle, Ely corrected himself, seeing the annotation indicating the man was married. Carlisle had retaliated but neither quickly nor forcefully enough. Before he had landed two blows, Lundy had managed five. Carlisle went down.

And there, Ely thought, the fight could have ended. It would have ended if the woman, now kneeling next to the unconscious Mr Carlisle, hadn't picked up a chair and swung it into Lundy's back.

Ely winced as he replayed footage of that blow. It might be a spinal injury. He hoped not. That would mean months of rehabilitation, possibly even a year before the man was productive once more.

The evidence was incontestable. Once Lundy was down the woman had swung the chair at his head, twice. There was no question that this warranted a custodial sentence. The only possible mitigating factor lay in the reason why she'd gone to the aid of Mr Carlisle in the first place. Sadly, Ely thought he already knew.

"You picked up that chair and hit him. Why?" Ely asked the woman.

She raised her eyes from the man on the floor.

"Because he..." she swallowed, and her tone became loud and defiant. "Because he hit Gerald. My husband."

Ely nodded. The display recorded her name as Mrs Geraldine Carlisle. The two had been approved for breeding three days ago, registered their marriage during their next free shift, and officially changed their names twenty minutes later.

Marriage wasn't compulsory, nor was changing one's name, but both were strongly encouraged since the Re-Organisation. Adopting the names of old places now lost beneath the waves was a way of holding onto the past, of remembering those billions who had died, and carrying their memory onwards to Mars. That was what Councillor Cornwall had said. Ely didn't disagree with the policy - he'd adopted one of the old names himself - he just didn't understand the importance of it. Not that it mattered to his job. A citizen could change their name everyday, but that wouldn't stop the system from tracking their every waking moment.

"Why were you here this evening?" he asked Mrs Carlisle.

"Why shouldn't I be?" she retorted.

"A good citizen like you, why weren't you in Recreation?"

"We already did our time there," she said.

Ely checked the records.

"It says here that you did two hours," he said.

There was a murmur of disapproval from the crowd.

"So? It's not like it's compulsory," she stated belligerently.

"No, it's not. And the only reason it's not is that most workers know to do their duty. All we need is for each worker to spend four of their off-shift hours exercising on one of the machines in the Recreation Room, and we'll generate enough electricity to keep the Tower working. And the only reason that malingerers like you don't cause the lights to turn off is that most people do five or more."

There was a mixture of self-righteous nodding of heads and shame-faced downcasting of eyes from the crowd.

The Tower's citizens were split into three shifts. Whilst one third worked, one third slept, and another third were free to do what they wanted. Each shift lasted approximately seven hours, with an hour in between for the workers to get from one part of the Tower to another. During that time, the drones cleaned and sanitised the Assemblies, 'homes' and lounges, getting them ready for the next shift.

Theoretically, every citizen had seven hours each day to do with as they pleased. And they had, up until fifteen years ago. That was when the rains had begun.

Whether the rising seas had brought the rains, or the deluge had caused the flood, no one knew. That the water had risen up to lap at the walls outside Level Three, and that the constant rain made the solar panels useless, was indisputable.

"You changed your name to that of your husband," Ely said to Mrs Carlisle. "Indeed, you chose to get married, yet you waste all this energy here when you should be contributing to the greater good. I find that suspiciously inconsistent."

"They were celebrating," the man with the broken arm, Roger Grimsby spat out.

"Celebrating what?" Ely asked, but again, he thought already knew.

"That we were going to be able to have a child," Mrs Carlisle stammered, her defiance beginning to crack under the withering stares of the mob.

"See?" Grimsby said with zealous indignation, "That's as good as treason. Production must come first, that's what Councillor Cornwall says, and he's right. People like them," he spat again, "they have no thought for the future, no thought about the society as a whole. All they care about is themselves."

"Quiet!" Ely barked, as he quickly ran through the footage working out Grimsby's part in it.

Lundy had knocked Mr Carlisle to the ground, but not knocked him out. Ely watched as Grimsby waded into the melee, shoving Mrs Carlisle out of the way. The woman blocked his view. He switched to a different camera. He saw Grimsby kick Mr Carlisle in the head. Ely pulled up the footage from Grimsby's visor and replayed the scene. He was clearly responsible for knocking the man out. The question was whether that kick was intentional.

"We just wanted to spend time together," Mrs Carlisle said, this time quietly.

The tutting from the crowd, now collectively relieved that their sins were minor compared to hers, grew.

"What use are children?" Grimsby asked, sensing that he had the support of the mob. "That's just more unproductive mouths to feed. And what use is that when we're so close to leaving the Earth? Seventeen years is what it takes to breed someone up until they can be productively useful. That's a seventeen-year drain on resources. How does that help when the first ship will launch in a year's time? Can't you wait?"

"Seventeen years, plus the two weeks maternity leave for her," Juliana Dundee said, seeking to gain some of the crowd's favour. "And count the energy lost in running the crèche and the school. We'd be on Mars already if it weren't for the likes of them."

Whether to have a moratorium on population increase was a debate that had been raging since the launch date had been announced, and one Ely expected to continue until the last human stepped off the planet for the last time.

"And what," he asked the crowd loudly, "about the two people we will now have to breed up as replacements for these two who are going to the hospital? You didn't think about that, did you? No, I've seen the footage. You can spout whatever high-minded rhetoric you want, but none of you were acting in the interests of production."

That shut them up.

He glanced down at Mr Carlisle. The injured man was looking increasingly pale. It was possible, Ely thought, that the nurses wouldn't arrive in time.

"Dundee, for damaging state property I'm docking you sixty points. Leeds, Ashford, for wilful assault you're docked forty points each. As for the rest of you, none of you tried to stop the brawl. That makes you equally culpable. I could dock each and every one of you for the loss of labour," he paused, "but I won't. I'm inclined to be lenient. I'm docking you twenty points each."

Ely looked from person to person to see if anyone would argue. No one said a word. Most looked resigned, some indifferent, others dismayed, their reactions determined by how many points they'd had at the start of the shift. He tapped out a command, logging the sentences, and then distributed them to each citizen.

"You have a right to appeal," he said, formally. "Appeals must be lodged within the next twenty-four hours. Failure to appeal will be taken as an admission of guilt." He paused for a moment before continuing. "This lounge is now closed until shift-change. It will require hours of labour to repair the damage you've caused." It wouldn't. The drones would have it cleaned and ready for the next shift in under thirty minutes. "It's only fitting, therefore, that you go now and queue for your 'home', and," he added as there was a whisper of grumbling from the back of the crowd, "I suggest you go now, before I change my mind about the charges."

The grumbling grew louder as they headed out the doors. Ely ignored them.

As the last of the mob left the lounge, Tower-One's two nurses, Bronwin Gower and Geoffrey Bradford entered, each pushing a stretcher before them. Like the other civic servants, their material-efficient jumpsuit was dyed blue, though of a lighter shade than the one Ely wore.

Nurse Bradford moved to the men on the floor, whilst Nurse Gower moved straight to Grimsby, whose moaning, Ely thought, was louder and more theatrical than before.

"It's fractured, but not badly," Nurse Gower said. "You'll need a cast. Can you walk?"

"I don't know," Grimsby replied, his voice weak.

"I thought you said you were for Production First," Ely snapped. "And now you want us to waste more hours pushing you up to the infirmary."

"Alright, I can walk," Grimsby said, getting to his feet with an exaggerated show of discomfort. Ely smiled at the nurse in a gesture of knowing solidarity.

"Good," she said, ignoring the Constable. "Then make your own way over to the elevators. We'll meet you there shortly."

"How long will you need to treat him?" Ely asked, loudly.

The nurse made a point of taking her time in answering.

"Transferring the other two will take half an hour," she said. "Call it two hours. Perhaps three."

Ely nodded and checked the time. It was two hours until the end of shift. During shift-change the elevators were reserved for the sole use of workers.

"I'll be up half an hour after shift-change to sentence him," he said.

Sentencing Grimsby could wait. Sentencing Mrs Carlisle could not.

"Mrs Geraldine Carlisle, for your active part in the hospitalisation of two workers and the loss of production that will cause, I sentence you to death." The woman didn't even flinch. She knew what was coming. "However, due to the current labour shortage of which you are now a cause, and if you waive the right to appeal, I am inclined to give you a choice. Death or 100,000 hours service on the penal gangs at the launch site. The choice is yours."

"Some choice! 100,000 hours? How long is that? Thirty years?"

"It's still a choice," Ely said. "For the record, do you accept the sentence or do you wish to appeal?"

"Fine, fine. I'll accept," she said despondently. "What does it matter? I won't be having any children, will I?"

"Not now, no."

"But, perhaps we will," she said, her defiance returning once more, "when we get to Mars."

"Perhaps," he allowed. "The punishment will be ratified when you reach Tower-Thirteen."

He turned to Nurse Bradford who was bent over two unconscious men.

"How are they?" the Constable asked.

"There's nothing we can do for them here," the male nurse replied. "They need the hospital. Did you remember to call Tower-Thirteen for a transport?"

"I can't," Ely said slowly, through gritted teeth, "not until you confirm it's necessary. That's procedure."

"Well, I'm confirming it now," the nurse retorted.

"Control," Ely said, turning his back on the nurses and injured felons, "I'm confirming we have two patients who need emergency transport to Tower-Thirteen. One felon is being transported with them, her sentence is to be ratified at the prison."

"Of course," Vauxhall said. "What about the man with the injured arm? He doesn't look too serious."

"You're watching?" Ely glanced up at the nearest camera.

"Of course. It's not like there's anything else going on in the Tower right now."

Conscious that everything was being recorded, and knowing that a Constable was far more easily replaced than a Controller, Ely kept his remarks strictly professional.

"That man, Grimsby, can be treated in the infirmary," he said.

"Fine. Transport for three," she said with a tone that Ely thought didn't match the gravity of the situation. He didn't comment. Nor did he say anything to the two nurses as they loaded the injured felons onto the stretchers and pushed them out through the doors with Mrs Carlisle following close behind.

Another thought struck him. The nurses might be able to treat Grimsby in the infirmary, but that didn't mean the man would be able to continue working with his arm in a cast. He pulled up footage from the man's last shift. Ely relaxed again as he watched Grimsby work.

A piece of circuitry came in across the conveyor and stopped. The man bent over it, a thin metal wand in his right hand. He touched it against a piece of wire. A light on the wand turned green, the conveyor belt moved, taking the now-approved component up to the sorting room on Level Seventy-Seven where it would await collection and transportation. Ely didn't bother to check what the circuitry was being used for. It didn't matter. Grimsby could perform his duties with one hand.

Ely looked around the now empty lounge. The place was a mess, but no more so than usual. He stepped outside and swiped his hand down the panel on the wall. The door closed. He tapped out a command, and a moment later he heard the sound of the drones coming out of their concealed crevices to clean and sanitise the room.

He tapped out a requisition for a new chair. He doubted it would be approved. Almost as an afterthought, he tapped out another message, placing a requisition for a new helmet. He doubted that would get approved either.

A green light blinked at the bottom of his vision. He had a call coming in. It was from Chancellor Stirling. He answered.

"Yes ma'am."

"Why aren't you on patrol, Constable?"

"There was a disturbance in the—"

"I know that. You think I wouldn't know?" she interrupted. "You've sentenced the suspects. Whilst this might have been the most serious incident in some time, the crime is now over. I can see that. What I can't see is why you are not on patrol."

"I'd finished my shift and was on Recreation when I was alerted to the —" but again she didn't let him finish.

"The police need to be seen," she said. "I've told you this. Or do you think I can be disregarded, eh? The election hasn't occurred yet, Constable. I am still Chancellor. Useful workers, productive workers, vital citizens..." she put an emphasis on the words to make it clear she did not count Ely as one of them, "...need to know that the energy they expend to ensure your comfort is well spent. Justice needs to be seen to be done, so go and be seen, Constable."

"Yes ma'a..." But she had already clicked off.

Ely briefly closed his eyes. In just over a day the election would begin. It didn't matter what she said, Stirling was going to lose and Cornwall would replace her.

Four years ago Cornwall had been a worker in Tower-Four. There was an explosion in one of the Factories and Cornwall had run into the fire to rescue the components from inside. That was a week before the election. During the aftermath, when various citizens approached him looking for a story to post to the newsfeeds, he gave his speech on Re-Organisation. He spoke of remembering the past but focusing on the future, on putting Production First as the only way to ensure humanity reached Mars. The sentiment, and his heroics, struck a chord with the electorate. Though he wasn't an official candidate, when it came to vote over 80,000 people, nearly eighty percent of the City's voting age population, wrote his name onto their ballot.

Chancellor Stirling, re-elected by the slimmest of margins, then adopted his policy of Re-Organisation. Everyone saw through this transparent attempt to benefit from Cornwall's popularity. The Chancellor's poll numbers had been sinking steadily ever since.

Ely was an avid supporter of Councillor Cornwall and his theories of Production First. It was his aim to one day follow the man into politics and become a Councillor himself. Though he doubted whether anyone would vote for someone as universally reviled as a Constable.

Putting thoughts of sleep on hold, at least for a few more hours, he walked over to the elevator to begin his lonely patrol.

He started up in the classrooms of Level Seventy-Five. Ely opened the door quietly, and began to walk slowly between the rows of desks.

"The City of Britain has a population of 159,097." The Instructor pointed to each word on the screen as he read the sentence out. Most of the class, aged between six and nine, struggled with the stylus as they copied down the words as best they could.

"The City of Rights has a population of 143,890," the Instructor continued. Ely tried not to smile as he walked past a girl battling over the direction the letter 'R' should face.

Ely's fingers twitched with reflexive guilt. He'd not practiced with a stylus since he'd left school at seventeen. Writing was one of the key skills, not necessary to everyday life now but which would be essential on Mars. Even the most optimistic estimates predicted there would be a decade's long gap between the current stock of wristboards and screens wearing out and the colonists establishing the mining and processing industries needed to replace them.

"And The People's City has a population of 128,700," the Instructor finished. "Now calculate the total number of humans left on the planet."

A hand went up.

"Yes, girl?" the Instructor snapped.

"Please sir, does that count the people working on the launch site? Or is it just the people living in the Towers?"

The Instructor's nostrils flared.

"Stupid girl! What have I told you about thinking before raising your hand? With four thousand people on each shift and with thirteen Towers in the City, there wouldn't be enough 'homes' to go around if that didn't include the people striving at the launch site."

"Sorry sir," the girl muttered. She bent her head, her cheeks flushed with embarrassment as some of the more daring students sniggered.

"Silence!" the Instructor bellowed. There was a sudden shuffling as the class buried their heads in a show of studious calculation.

Ely allowed himself a smile. Fifteen years before, he'd been sitting in one of those very same desks, and he'd been the one to ask that very same question. He didn't recall if he'd had the same Instructor. He was tempted to check, but the right hand side of his display was currently filled with the paperwork from the incident in the lounge.

Paperwork. That was one of the many words that had stuck with them from the old world. No one had made any paper since the Great Disaster sixty years before. Very little of anything was made except that which was needed for the ships. Technology had frozen, stuck at the level when the wars began all those decades ago.

As he continued his slow walk around the classroom, he returned his attention to the recordings of the brawl. For each felon that he'd sentenced he had to find two pieces of camera footage, each from a different angle, to add to the file as evidence. Unless one of the citizens lodged an appeal, something that hadn't happened in his five years as a Constable, those files would never be opened again. Nonetheless, the laws had to be followed. The City of Britain was a nation of laws. It was written into the Constitution and always had been. That was what Ely had been told.

He completed his circuit and made his way out into the corridor and along to the next classroom. There he got a disapproving glare from the Instructor as the students, all aged twelve to sixteen, turned to see who had come in.

"Eyes to the front. Now! A faulty wire might cause the entire ship to explode!" The Instructor kept her eyes on Ely as she said it. He didn't care. Under his helmet and behind his visor, his expression was unreadable. The Instructor went back to reading out a speech, and the class went back to copying it down.

Ely listened long enough to gather it had something to do with how to create oxygen through electrolysis, then went back to collating the evidence. He'd tagged another two felons by the time his slow walk had brought him to the front of the classroom.

"If the first ship brings 1,000 people," the Instructor intoned, "the second 10,000, then calculate our total oxygen requirement before the second ship has returned to Earth. I will award a bonus point to the first student who can calculate the energy requirement for scrubbing the carbon dioxide from the air."

Heads bowed and frantic calculations began.

Ely had hated his time in school. He'd hated it almost as much as the six months he'd worked on the Assemblies before Arthur appointed him Constable. He hated coming back, shift after shift, just to show the uniform of authority. He left the classroom and looked down the corridor. Opposite were the classrooms for the older children, with their more rigorous technical training. Further along was the crèche, and beyond that, the nursery. Ely imagined he could already hear the crying. He decided he'd been seen enough on that level. He turned and walked back towards the elevator.

On the level above the classrooms was the museum and the Twilight Room, home to the retirees who volunteered to stay in Tower-One. Ely didn't need to patrol there. Arthur, his former supervisor and the oldest of the retirees still living in Tower-One, kept a close eye on that level.

Above that was Level Seventy-Seven, home to Councillor Cornwall and his two assistants, the infirmary and the transportation pad. The Councillor had made it clear that he wasn't to bother patrolling up there.

Ely tapped a command into his wristboard, and the elevator descended to the food-vats. Since the Re-Organisation, everyone was supposed to call them 'farms'. It was meant to train people to think more like future settlers and less like prisoners trapped in the Towers on a world their ancestors had made uninhabitable. Ely still thought of them as the vats, for that was what they were. Each grew a different type of algae that some old world scientist had genetically engineered to be rich in vitamins, proteins, or carbohydrates. Once grown, they were processed, dried and turned into a fine powder. That was piped to the dispensers in the 'homes', lounges and break-rooms, ready to be mixed with water and flavouring according to each workers own personal taste. To Ely, no matter what was done with it, it still tasted like a flavourless, textureless, gloop.

He exited the elevator, walked along the hallway, and peered through the small window to the first 'farm'. He didn't go in. He didn't need to. The vats were almost entirely automated. Only thirty people per shift worked in the 'farms', their job being to check that the numbers on the gauges matched the figures the system gathered from the array of sensors lining nearly every inch of every vat.

In turn, the system used the scores of cameras in the room to monitor the workers. Each citizen had been trained to perform their task with a specific series of movements, each in a specific order, to ensure maximum accuracy and efficiency. Should a worker deviate from their set routine, the system would send them a warning. If it were to happen twice within a shift, their supervisor would be alerted. Only if it happened three times in a shift would Ely be notified. That hadn't happened in two years. On that occasion, it was due to a worker collapsing from a brain aneurism halfway through a shift.

Ely began to walk slowly down the corridor, peering into room after room, pausing at each window just long enough to be noticed by the supervisor.

Each year, two hundred and ten people were bred. No, Ely corrected himself, they were *born*, that was the term they were supposed to use now. They spent the first year in the nursery, then two in the crèche, before they began their formal schooling. That lasted until they were seventeen when they joined the workforce. If Councillor Cornwall was elected Chancellor, everyone expected the age for graduation would be reduced to fourteen. Factoring in the Instructors, the two weeks of maternity leave that each mother now received, and the energy and food cost of so many unproductive mouths, the population rate was one of the most contentious issues in the City.

Not that two hundred and ten people died every year. Some retired to Tower-Thirteen. Others were transferred to one of the other Towers or were sentenced to hard labour at the launch site. And sometimes there would be calls for volunteers to assist them. That had happened twice last year.

Few people just died with the random lack of forethought that the man who had dropped dead in the food-vats had exhibited. Most died in their sleep, just like the records showed they had done in the old world.

An image of Mrs Carlisle came up on his screen. Ely agreed with most of Cornwall's policies, but felt that some workers used the breeding licences as a way to get out of Recreation. That was the case with the Carlisles, he decided. They were two people who'd had some chance meeting and decided they'd have children for the perks that parenthood brought. Had they both not already lost their licence, he would have been inclined to put in a motion to have it rescinded.

He took another turning and found himself back at the elevator. He went down to the Assemblies. As with the food-vats, he would be alerted if there was an incident he needed to attend. Unlike with the 'vats, Ely wasn't allowed inside except in a dire emergency. The Assemblies were clean rooms. As Ely knew, as everyone knew, the merest speck of dirt could cause a circuit board to fail. If that happened in the depths of space the entire ship might be lost, imperilling the hopes of the species. Or, as the digital poster outside the room stated, 'Dirt Kills! Are you clean?'

As Ely looked in through the window a worker glanced up. It was hard to read an expression underneath that mask, but Ely knew what it was. Frustrated anger at the waste of labour Ely represented.

The supervisor, alerted by the sudden drop in productivity, hurried over to the worker. The citizen returned his gaze to the piece of circuitry on his conveyor belt. Then it was the supervisor's turn to glare at Ely.

Ely shifted his helmet, trying to find a position where its new dent didn't pinch the back of his close-cropped head. It would only take a few minutes to print a new one, and barely longer to transfer the visor and other electronics from the old one, but he would have to wait until the requisition was approved. If it was approved.

Every joule of energy, every minute of labour, now had to be accounted for. More and more workers were needed at the launch site, and that meant fewer and fewer people in the Towers, yet the workload remained the same. Ely knew it and secretly shared the frustration of that worker - that he, as a Constable, was nothing but an extra mouth to be fed.

For sixty years everyone in all three of humanity's remaining cities had been striving towards the same goal, the evacuation of the species to Mars. The focus had been so intense that few workers had given much thought to the struggles that would face them once they arrived. There, survival would be reliant on the technologies developed long ago, before the Great Disaster.

Those, Ely knew, had never been tested outside of the lab. Terraforming, agriculture, mining, and so much more besides, it would all have to be experimented with, and it would all have to work. There would be no room for failure. Nor could there be any delay in departure. The water levels were still rising. The City had no more than ten years left.

The situation had not always been so desperate. Fifteen years ago, whilst Ely had been a student in that classroom, the sun had shone outside. But it had shone on a barren lifeless land, plagued by the stray winds that brought toxic gasses with them from the old battlefields to the north. Thanks to the solar panels, no matter how inhospitably desolate it was, energy had been abundant.

Then the rains began, and the solar panels failed. The sea levels rose, and the tunnels connecting the Towers, rarely used since the years immediately after the Great Disaster, were flooded. The transport pads became the only way to move people and supplies between the Towers and Cities.

There was an energy crisis. Workers from Tower-Thirteen were re-assigned to construct a giant tidal barrier to hold back the sea and harness the power of the waves. Most of them died in the process but the barrier was built and the sea kept at bay, for a time. It had begun to rise again, and it was estimated that within a decade the barriers would fail, the Towers would be swamped, and everyone would die. Mars had become humanity's only hope.

Ely moved on, pausing at the empty break area where workers spent their statutory fifteen-minute lunch break. He checked. It had been six hours since his last meal. He was eligible for another. He took out a cup and placed it under the dispenser. A thin, gloopy liquid poured out of the nozzle. He downed the gruel in one gulp. Unlike some of the citizenry, he saw no reason to savour it.

Cornwall had been responsible for extending the break time to a quarter of an hour. Ely sometimes thought that the man's policies were coloured by the time he had spent as a worker in the Factories.

Looking down the long corridor at door after door, Ely decided he was wasting his time. He returned to his paperwork. Once he was finished, he could sentence Grimsby then go and get his four hours sleep.

Unlike the workers, Ely didn't have much free time. Civic servants didn't work a shift pattern, but spent fourteen hours on duty. He tried to fit in six hours of Recreation each day, he felt that at least that way he wasn't a net drain of energy on the Tower. It wasn't always possible.

That only left four hours for sleep. Though the workers were told that six hours per day was needed, Ely knew that only four hours of the machine induced lucid sleep was technically required. Technically.

He liked Recreation. Like everyone else, as he peddled away turning calories into electricity, he had his eyes glued to his display, lost in the movies, reading the books, and scanning the archives that had survived from the old world.

Ely had seen every one of the four hundred and ninety-eight films that had survived often enough to know every line that each actor spoke. He'd found it odd that since all their technology came from the old world, and that all the screens in the Tower had colour displays, no one had thought to make colour movies. It was equally odd that none of them portrayed the technology that he was familiar with. He had a theory about that, connected with the old world's strict censorship during a time of war. He hoped, some day, that he'd find time to write a paper on it. All the successful political candidates had contributed pieces to the archives in Tower-Thirteen. He sighed. It wouldn't be anytime soon.

An alert came up on his display. The shift was about to change. Ely moved to the side of the hallway. Doors opened, the workers began to file out, and head towards the ramps.

The Tower had ten elevators, each capable of carrying fifty workers at a time, though they only ever carried most of them up from the 'homes' to the Assemblies, 'farms' or classrooms at the beginning of the shift. Around the lift shafts at the centre of the Tower were the commuter ramps. It was down these, during shift-change, that the workers walked, queued, and waited for the previous shift to move on from rest to sleep. They talked, they joked, and they ignored Ely. He stood there, silently, his hand moving to check boxes, clicking yes or no, as he filled away a dozen more reports.

When he'd become a Constable, nearly five years ago, there had been no patrolling. Life then had been exciting, though he'd not thought so at the time. He and Tower-One's other two Constables, under the gaze of their supervisor, Arthur, would pour through the other-net, seeking out sedition and recidivism. There had been an arrest a week, sometimes two, always resulting in deportation to the launch site.

That had gone with the election of Councillor Cornwall and the Chancellor's adoption of his policy of Re-Organisation. Two Constables from each Tower, along with dozens of Instructors and nurses and other civic servants, were sent to the launch site. Arthur was forced into retirement on Level Seventy-Six, and Ely was left to patrol the Tower alone.

Work, rest, repeat. That was life for everyone in the Tower, and it was the same for every worker in every Tower of each of the three Cities left on Earth. Three hundred thousand souls, all following the same routine, all dreaming of the day that...

A light began flashing on his display. There was a disturbance outside a hab-unit down on Level Six. No, Ely reminded himself as he brought up the camera feed from the corridor in question, they were called 'homes' now. The image from outside the 'home' showed two couples arguing, with two sets of children loitering disinterestedly behind them, lost in the worlds behind their displays

It didn't look serious, and though all had elevated heart rates, the system suggested there was a low probability of violence.

Mentally, Ely cursed. During shift-change the elevators were to only be used by the workers. That was another one of Chancellor Stirling's edicts, one Ely suspected she had directed at him personally. He could use the long winding commuter corridor, but he didn't want to endure the baleful gaze of all those citizens. He walked over to the nearest access ladder and began the long climb down to Level Six.

Chapter 1 - The First Murders
Twenty-four hours before the election

"Alright, move along, move along," Ely called out when he rounded the corridor. Other family groups, all the same two-parent, two-child variety, were lingering outside their allocated rooms.

"Go on, get to your beds," he said, pushing a woman towards her hab-unit. "An hour's lost sleep is an hour's lost production."

The trite slogan, one of Chancellor Stirling's that Ely disliked on principle, had the desired effect. The crowd began to move, not into their 'homes' where they would miss out on this latest piece of entertainment, but close enough to the doors that they could bolt inside should the threats be directed at any of them personally.

"So," he said, reaching the group at the centre of the disturbance, "what seems to be the trouble?"

"Constable. Finally! Can you tell these *people* that Wisteria Lodge is our home?" The man spoke in clipped tones, every other word punctuated with scornful impatience. According to the tag on Ely's display, he was Mr George Winchester, an assessor in one of the Assemblies. His wife, Mrs Georgette Winchester, was an overseer in the same Assembly. Their two children, a boy aged twelve, a girl aged eight, stood to one side.

In front of the doors to the unit in question, with their children loitering to the side, stood another equally exasperated married couple. Ely's display tagged them as Mr Alfred and Mrs Alfreda Durham.

"Look, please," Mrs Durham said. "We're tired. We're *all* tired. We just want to go to bed."

"Well, what of it?" Georgette Winchester snapped. "So do we. And we can't, because you won't let us into our home."

"But we keep telling you," Mr Durham said, "it's our home this shift."

"He's right," Mrs Durham agreed. "It is. It's ours!"

"Quiet. All of you," Ely barked. He was tired. His throat felt sore after all the shift's shouting. His head still throbbed from the blow that had dented his helmet. Above all, his pride was bruised from the conversation with Chancellor Stirling.

"And the rest of you," he said, addressing the workers dawdling further along the corridor, "get to bed. An hour's lost sleep is an hour's lost production. Anyone still out here in five seconds will be fined a point for that lost hour." This time the workers fled into their units.

"As for you," he said addressing the two sets of adults, "stay quiet or I'll charge you with disturbing the peace."

They glared but stayed silent as Ely tapped a command onto his wristboard and brought up the hab-unit allocation for that shift.

"Unit 6-4-18 is allocated to the Winchesters," he said, imbuing his voice with finality. Both sets of adults looked at him blankly. Ely stared back for a moment, then he sighed. "I mean Wisteria Lodge," he amended.

"See?" Mrs Winchester crowed. "I told you."

"The Durhams are assigned to..." Unit 6-4-17. "... Sea View. Next one down," Ely said, and closed the file.

"Yes, yes." Mr Durham made no attempt to move. "I know that's what it says." He waved his wrist at Ely. "But that door won't open. It says it's already occupied. And I know how it works. If a 'home' is occupied, everyone moves down one. That means that this one..." he tapped on the door. "...is ours."

That wasn't how it worked. Units were sometimes unavailable. It was rare, but sometimes a pod needed replacing, the printer needed resetting or the plumbing needed fixing. It was rare, but it did happen, and when it did the 'home' was removed from the night's roster.

According to the records on Ely's display, Unit 6-4-17 was meant to be available for that shift. He checked the data. There were no signs of life from inside. The room had to be empty. He assumed it was a glitch. There had been a few of those recently, though none so great as this.

"You two, get out of the way," he snapped at the Durhams. "Now! Or..." he tried to think of a threat, "Or I'll dock you a point each for every minute of the Winchesters' sleep that you disrupt." He lowered his hand to hover over his wristboard. The couple moved.

Ely turned to the Winchesters, "Go inside. Go to sleep."

"Finally!" Mr Winchester sighed. He waved his hand down the scanner. The door opened, and the family traipsed into the room. None of them offered a word of thanks.

"This way," Ely said to the Durhams, and walked the dozen feet down the corridor to Unit 6-4-17.

"Look, Constable. It's pointless. The door won't open." Mrs Durham swiped her hand down the scanner. A small red light flashed. Ely was able to see the message on her wristboard display that read 'home occupied'. She swiped her hand down the panel again. The message changed, now reading 'Please check your assignment'.

On Ely's display a different message came up 'Attempted unauthorised entry to Unit 6-4-17'.

It was definitely a glitch. A big one. More hours of production would be wasted whilst it was fixed. He checked the time. It was twenty minutes past shift-change. The family inside would already have left.

"Control, come in."

"Constable?"

"We've a malfunction on Unit 6-4-17. It's registering as in use. Can you check on the location of the previous occupants?"

"Sure. That was... the Greenes. Alphonse and Finnya, and two children, Simon aged eleven and Beatrice aged nine. The children are both logged as having had breakfast and are on their way up to school."

"And the parents?" Ely asked.

"They're..." He had to wait whilst she ran a scan of the Tower's occupants. "... not showing up. Anywhere. That's odd."

Ely frowned. It was more than odd. As far as he knew, it was impossible.

He tapped out a command, bringing up the image from the camera inside the unit. The screen was blank.

"Control," he began, but Mr Durham interrupted him.

"How long is this going to take?" the man asked.

Ely glanced over at him and his family.

"We need our sleep," Mrs Durham said, then almost as an afterthought added, "Our children need their sleep. Like you said, an hour's lost sleep is an hour's lost production."

Ely regretted having used that slogan.

He thought quickly. Grimsby was still up in the infirmary. The Carlisles, with no children were still allocated to the 'Apartments', so was Lundy, and with those three now on their way to Tower-Thirteen, that meant four pods had suddenly become vacant. He tapped out a command, double-checked he was correct, and allocated those pods to the Durhams.

"I'm assigning you to Units 7-15-4, 7-18-6, 7-20-2 and 7-21-3," he said.

They looked at him blankly. He'd forgotten, again.

"Pine Lodge Apartments. Here." He tapped a command onto the screen at his wrist. "Follow the lights on your display."

"Apartments? We're a family. We're entitled to a family room," Mr Durham said.

"It's just for one night," Ely said then, remembering one of the Chancellor's recent edicts on 'civility and civic duty', added, "I do apologise."

"Just come on, Alfred," the daughter said. "I'm tired."

Interestingly, Ely noted, though she looked as if she was engrossed in her display, according to the system, it was switched off. He checked. She'd not turned it on since she'd left the classrooms. Ely flagged her details so the system would monitor the girl more closely. Deviation from the norm in youth was usually a sign of criminal recidivism in later life. He'd read that in one of the papers in the Tower's digital archive.

The parents relented and the family headed off towards the ramp that would lead them to the level above.

"Control," Ely asked, when they had gone, "can you give me a remote override on the door?"

There was a click as the locks disengaged. The narrow door slid open by half an inch. Ely pushed it into the recess in the wall.

The space inside was dark.

"Lights."

Nothing happened.

"Control. Lights."

"What? Oh sorry," the Controller, Vauxhall said. "I got distracted, there's a—"

"Just turn the lights on," he interrupted.

The lights came on.

Unit 6-4-17, just like every other family 'home', was twelve feet wide by ten feet deep by ten feet tall. On the left, stacked one on top of another, were the 'beds', a double pod for the parents, and two individual ones for the children. All were seven feet long and three-feet high. The two individual pods were three-feet wide. The double was seven-feet wide.

The moment that an occupant's head hit the small metal contacts in the cushioned pillow, a carefully modulated six and a half hours of lucid sleep would be induced. To get in or out the pods would lower and rotate according to the pre-programmed rota of who was scheduled to wake first, thus reducing congestion with the unit's basic facilities.

Ely had entered through the night-side door. Directly opposite was the day-side door. Workers always entered through the night-side, where the corridor lighting was subdued. They always exited through the day-side, where the corridor leading to the elevators was always bathed in a soft yellow-white glow.

To the right of the door were the shower, the toilet, the food-bar and the printer. The unit the Winchesters had gone into, 'Wisteria Lodge', was the mirror opposite but otherwise identical.

'Pine Lodge Apartments', to which he'd just sent the Durhams, had six individual pods per room. Those were modulated for only six hours of sleep per shift due to the extra demand on the shower, printer and toilet.

That extra half an hour of sleep was one of the benefits of having children, one that he personally thought was offset by having to share that pod with someone else.

"A place to sleep, not to live," was how Arthur described it. "Living's a luxury for the future, and our job is to make sure there's a future generation to enjoy it." For now people worked, and work should be enough.

The children's pods were empty, as Ely had expected. Neither had been sanitised. He glanced at the wall. A series of digital frames still showed the Greene family. One, a very popular picture at the moment, showed the four of them, all with fixed grins and glazed eyes, set against a reddish-dusty background of Mars. Underneath was a split frame. The right hand side showed a boy, Simon, sitting in a row with two dozen, much older children. His eyes obscured by a visor, his hands frozen in mid motion. On the left side of the frame was a piece captured from a newsfeed. '11 year old wins National Diligence Award.' There was a lot of text underneath, but it wasn't important. The pictures wouldn't change, nor would the pods be sanitised until a family, the whole family, had vacated the room. Ely thought he knew what had happened.

Conscious that he was only delaying the inevitable, he glanced over at the small shower and toilet cubicles. If they were in use, the doors would turn opaque. Both doors were transparent. It was as he'd expected. No one had ever died in the shower. That death in the Assembly had been rare. Most people died in their sleep, but two deaths in the same pod was unprecedented, and it couldn't have happened at a worst time. Five lost producers in one night.

There was no point putting it off any longer, he decided. He swiped his hand down a panel to the side of the pods. Nothing happened. Ely frowned. He tried again. The pods should have rotated, bringing the double unit down to eye-level.

"Control. Can you override all locks and doors in this room?"
There was a series of clicks. Ely grabbed the double-sleep-pod, pulled it out and down. The panel covering the top half of the unit was opaque. Taking a deep breath, he pressed the emergency release and pulled the top up and along.

The moment the seal was broken, the cover turned clear and Ely saw what was inside. There were two bodies, but they hadn't died in their sleep.

Their throats had been cut. Blood had pooled around their arms and necks. The wounds were identical, the cuts so deep that Ely saw flecks of white bone amidst the congealing blood. Looking down at those terrible wounds, there was no doubt in his mind. It was murder.

There hadn't been one as long as he'd been a Constable. He didn't recall there ever being one before, not since the Towers were sealed off from the outside world.

He pulled up the records for the couple, maximising them so they filled his display and hid from view the sight of the two bodies.

Alphonse and Finnya Greene. Married for twelve years. She'd taken his surname when they got married, but neither had changed their names during the Re-Organisation. It wasn't compulsory, of course, but the only other person Ely knew who hadn't adopted one of the old names was Arthur.

Perhaps there was a place called 'Greene', Ely thought, as he scanned through the rest of the couple's record. He knew he was just trying to distract himself, trying to avoid thinking about what was in front of him. He told himself to focus. Then he saw something else. Finnya Greene didn't wear a visor. Around ten percent of the City's population didn't. It was one of the few defects that couldn't be identified before birth. Some workers reported motion sickness, others were just incapable of managing the fine focusing skills required to operate the display. That wasn't the case with Finnya Greene. She had worn one up until six months ago.

And then Ely remembered the woman. Instinctively his eyes flicked to the corner of his display. The screens cleared and he saw her lifeless, almost wax-like face, and this time he knew where they had met before.

Six months ago he had been patrolling the Recreation Room. She had just finished five hours on one of the machines. Ely knew it was five hours, he'd checked afterwards. She had approached him and held out her visor. "I don't need it anymore," was all that she'd said. He'd taken it, more out of confusion than anything else, and then she had walked off before he'd thought to question her.

He'd ordered extra passive medical screenings, set up the system to monitor her activity on the social network, and had personally checked to see if she posted anything to the other-net. She hadn't. His hourly checks became daily, then weekly and then, when there had been no hint of deviation whatsoever, he had forgotten her.

She seemed to have gotten on with her life, and according to the records, she had done it happily despite being cut off from the full array of shared experience that the visor enabled.

He checked her work records. They were exemplary. So too were her husband's. He wore a visor, but had that same low level of social activity as his wife. Both had voted for Cornwall during the last election. Both were registered to vote for him again. That meant nothing. The current polls showed almost ninety-nine percent of Tower-One had already pre-registered their vote for Cornwall to be Chancellor.

Both victims had a low criminal probability. Ely knew that couldn't be correct, so he checked it again. But no, hers was at three percent, her husband at five percent. They should have had one of the highest in the Tower.

He glanced down, then away again quickly. He found it hard to look at the bodies. He'd seen corpses before. In the event of a death, he and the nurses received the same alert. But he'd never seen them like this.

He looked back at the wounds. The blood hadn't spread far. It had pooled around their necks. Was that normal? He tried to remember his training five years before.

He'd followed Arthur for a few days, learning how to use the display, how to monitor the other-net and what to do if he found evidence of sedition. There had been a few hours spent learning how to apprehend a felon. That had mostly consisted of the older man repeatedly throwing Ely halfway across an empty corridor. Most of the time had been spent learning how to complete the paperwork. Ely didn't think there had been any discussion of what to do if there was a murder. The only words of advice he remembered that even approached relevance were 'be thorough'.

He checked that his camera was recording. It was and had been since he'd entered the room. He tracked slowly up and down the bodies, checking that he had captured every inch of the pod. Then he turned around, recording the rest of the room. Nothing appeared immediately amiss, but the system would analyse everything he recorded. It was far more reliable than his eyes and would identify anything he overlooked. He turned back to the bodies. There would have to be an official report.

"The victims are Mr Alphonse Greene and Mrs Finnya Greene," he said, keeping his voice low and solemn, "Their throats have been cut. By a sharp blade. Probably pressed down against their throats."

Was that right? He leant forwards over the pod. Yes. There wasn't much room. The sides of the pod were too high for anyone to reach in and slash. How much strength would that have required? The blade had sunk to the bone, nearly decapitating the victims. It was the wrong question, he realised. The important one was why hadn't the killer just stabbed his two victims? He thought he had an answer.

"The method used was probably chosen due to the type and shape of the weapon," he said. And that seemed right. It didn't help him identify what that weapon had been, though.

"The murders both had to be committed quickly and in quick succession," he said. Once the pod lid was opened, the machine was turned off. At most it took only a minute for someone to wake, but surely no one could sleep whilst their spouse was being murdered next to them.

"The killer acted quickly," he repeated.

He turned to look at the pictures on the wall. The family seemed genuinely happy, genuinely close. That was unusual. It stirred something within him. He turned back to the pod, but not to the bodies.

The couple's two wristboards, and Alphonse Greene's visor, were still in the slot on the pod's side. Why had there been no alarm? Whilst awake, each citizen's position, health, and activity were monitored through the wristboard. Whilst they slept it was monitored by the pod itself. The moment that their vital signs dropped an alarm should have been sounded.

An alarm should have sounded when the door was opened, for surely it must have done when the killer came in to the room. The pods could be opened during the night, but only from the inside. In which case the worker's supervisor would be alerted, and their productivity monitored during their next shift. The only way to open it from the outside was to use the emergency release that he had just used. In that case Control would be alerted, and the pod would be unusable until the whole unit had been reset.

He turned slowly, looking around the room. Alerts should have been sent when the food-bar was unused, when they failed to print off their clothes for the day, or use their three minutes each of hot water.

"Control." The word caught in the back of his throat. He took a breath and spoke again. "Control, can you confirm whether there were any alarms sounded for Unit 6-4-17 last shift?"

"I don't remember any alerts last shift, except for that brawl."

"Can you check?"

"Fine... No. No alerts for that unit, but you would have received them if there were."

He knew that, but Ely had hoped that somehow the fault lay in his own wristboard.

"Why?" Vauxhall asked, "What's the problem?"

Ely took another breath.

"Mr and Mrs Greene are dead."

"Are you sure?" she asked. "There's nothing registering on my system."

"This wasn't natural causes," Ely interrupted. "This was murder."

There was a sharp intake of breath followed by a moment's long silence.

"Murder?" Vauxhall asked.

"No question. Haven't you got the feed from the camera in the room?"

"I've got the feed, but the image is blank," she said.

Ely remembered that he'd found the same thing when he was outside, but he'd been distracted by Mr Durham.

"I'm trying to rotate the camera," Vauxhall said, "but the image is still blank. Is the lens covered?"

"Just look at the image from my visor." He waited. "Vox? Can you see them?"

"I do," she said, her voice stilted. "Alright, what do you want me to do?"

That was a good question, and one Ely wished he could have asked her. He couldn't, not when everything he said and did was going to be scrutinised by Chancellor Stirling for the slimmest reason to dismiss him.

"We need to work out when this happened. No alerts were sent, but the pod was still opened." He glanced at the two doors to the unit. "Someone had to come in here. Find out when."

"And what are you going to do?"

"Just get started," he replied, evading the question.

Ely turned back to look at the camera situated above the door. For reasons of privacy there was only one in each unit. Though it was mounted on a moveable bracket, remotely operated by the Controller, it usually pointed straight ahead. This one was turned to face the wall.

Ely walked over to it, reached up and carefully moved it to face back in the room. The bracket was broken.

"That has to be deliberate," he murmured.

"Ely, come in," Vauxhall said.

"Vox, have you found out when the door opened?"

"Yes. Three a.m. shift-time."

"And which door? Night-side or day-side?"

"Night-side. The day-side door didn't open between the time the previous occupants left the shift before, and when Simon and Beatrice Greene left for school a few hours ago."

"Well, now we're getting somewhere. So, who came in?"

"No one."

"What do you mean?"

"Just what I say. No one came in. I've got no one registered moving around within fifty yards of the unit at that time."

"Well, did the door open at any other time?"

"No, just at three a.m."

Everyone wore a wristboard. Everyone. It was the only way of accessing the Tower's server, and through it the elevators, the printers, the food-bars, the workstations in the Assemblies, and the lesson materials in the classroom. Wherever a person went, their wristboard went, and that meant a citizen's movements were always tracked. There were no exceptions.

"Check again," Ely said. "The killer had to open the door to get into the room. The door opened at three a.m. So that had to be the killer." Just in time he stopped himself from turning that last sentence into a question. He did not want Chancellor Stirling thinking he was uncertain.

"I've checked and rechecked," Vauxhall said. "The door opened, then closed. A few minutes later it opened and closed again. But no one came in."

"Well, obviously someone—"

"I mean we've no data," she interrupted.

"How long, exactly, between the door closing and then opening again?"

"Three minutes, forty seconds."

"I see," Ely said. He looked between the door and the pods.

"Is there anything else?" Vauxhall cut in on his thoughts.

"Yes," he said, as he opened the door to the unit and stepped outside. "Start timing." He walked back inside and mimed rotating the pods. Then he mimed forcing the lid open. He didn't mime the next part, but imagined leaning over and forcing a blade down with all his strength, then ripping it up and down again onto the throat of the second victim. Then he mimed closing the pod, rotating it and walked back over to the door.

"How long was that?" he asked.

"Two minutes fifty-eight seconds," Vauxhall replied.

So it was possible. Ely felt some relief at that.

"And you say you've got no record of anyone entering the room?"

"No."

He wondered whether it was worth checking the worker's visor feeds from the previous evening. He decided it wasn't, not yet. Someone who was being that meticulous in their preparations would have thought to take the visor off.

"And no one in the corridor outside?"

"I told you—"

"And no alarms went off either?"

"No, Ely, I—"

"Well," he said, interrupting her again, "it seems clear enough. The killer has a way of disconnecting the alarms, and some way of stopping the system tracking their movement." The idea was unnerving. "But I bet they can't make themselves invisible. Check the cameras in the hallway outside. One of them must have caught the killer."

"Fine." She clicked off.

He began to track the camera along the floor and walls. He wasn't looking for anything in particular, but it would look more decisive than just staring at the bodies. He needed time to think.

There were so many questions, so many possibilities. In his experience crimes were easily solved. They only ever required checking the system to log a citizen's position, and then checking the cameras to confirm the evidence against them. The implication of their being no record and no alarms sounded was so far beyond his experience that he found the notion terrifying.

With nothing else upon which to draw inspiration, he turned his mind to the old movies he loved so much. Fourteen of them dealt with murders, all of resistance fighters in The War. In those, the killers were always depicted as having some form of psychological defect. That can't be the case here. Psychosis had been bred out of the population. Those who exhibited deviation in later life were sent for rehabilitation. Of course, it was Ely's responsibility to spot those deviations. Clearly, he had failed.

Two bodies. Two victims, he had to remind himself. Except when he looked at them he saw the loss of fourteen shifts per week, fifty-two weeks per year. It would take nine months and seventeen years before they could be replaced.

The number '90,764 hours' came up on his display. He hadn't realised he'd been talking out loud. Add to that the two felons on the way to the hospital and the one on her way to the prison, and that worked out at over a quarter of a million hours lost to Tower-One in just one night. And that was before taking into account the extra resources that replacing personnel demanded. That gave him an idea.

"Vox?"

"Yes, Constable?"

"Were there any transports from the other Towers last night?"

"The one you ordered to take those workers to the hospital has just left. Before that there was one that collected food to be shipped to the launch site. That was... thirty hours ago."

"Right. But you've got the airlock feed? Could anyone have left the Tower unnoticed?"

"The nurses were there during transfer." Since the Re-Organisation, and since they were rarely busy, the nurses were responsible for the transfers of people and materials to and from Tower-One. "They would have noticed. Why?"

"I'm just reducing the number of possible suspects," Ely said. The killer had to be someone from Tower-One. That was a start.

Next, he decided to eliminate the obvious. He brought up the records for the two children. Both were in class, both were busy transcribing notes on how to repair hydroponics systems. He opened their activity logs. The daughter, Beatrice, had woken first. She'd showered, printed her clothes for the day and ordered breakfast from the food-bar. She'd selected the purple flavour, he idly noted. She'd then waited whilst her brother showered, dressed and ate. Together they'd gone to queue for the elevator to take them up to the classrooms. Again, he noted how close they were. It was unusual, but the more he learnt about the Greenes the more unusual they seemed.

He checked the records for the pods. Both children had slept through the entire night. Considering their current activity, he decided that they weren't involved in the crime.

He went back to check the records from the previous evening. The children had met their parents in Lounge-Three, what was now called The King's Arms. It was a popular place for families, partly because it kept them away from the increasingly resentful gaze of those workers who were single. They had eaten, talked - and again Ely wished that the microphones were still on - then gone onto Recreation. The children had completed four and a half hours, then gone to loiter in one of the corridors with some other children. The parents had completed five hours before going to join them. The family had returned to Lounge-Three, talked for another hour, and then gone to queue up, twenty minutes early, for Unit 6-4-17. And as they waited, they kept on talking. Ely wondered what they had talked about.

It wasn't the children. Nor had the parents had any contact with anyone else the previous evening that might have precipitated such a violent end.

He brought up the messages that the parents had received over the past week. He was surprised by how few there were. They were mostly the usual newsfeed articles and political broadcasts that filled Ely's own inbox each shift.

By law each candidate, even in a race with such a foregone conclusion as this one, had to communicate directly with the electorate. The same law required that each citizen read or watch each message. Judging by the length of time the message was open, and how long it took to scroll down the page, the Greenes actually had read them, or diligently pretended to.

The soft whine of the air-cycler brought him back to the present. The room would be needed for the next shift. He would have to find time, later, to go through the family's activity more carefully.

"Control, come in."

"I haven't anything for you yet, Constable," Vauxhall said, testily.

"I've something else for you to add to your list."

"What?"

"I want you to tag everyone that the Greenes came in contact with."

"Since when?"

"Let's start with this week and go back..." Yes, he thought. "... six months. The killer had to have known the victims," he added for the benefit of the recording.

"Fine. But I can only do one thing at a time." She clicked off before Ely could ask her anything else.

He looked again at the pod, then at the door to the night-side, then at the door to the day-side, and then down at the floor. It was clean, he realised. He opened the night-side door and stepped out into the corridor again.

"Control."

"Oh, what now?"

"Turn the lights in the night-side corridor on full."

They snapped on, turning the dimly light hallway brighter than day. It took a moment for Ely's eyes to adjust. He peered down at the floor.

After the brief training period, Arthur had given Ely access to the library's collection of forensics and criminology books. He had started to read all four, but the language had been so archaic, the content referencing so many things outside of his own experiences he'd not finished any of them. He'd found some of the academic papers easier to read. In one of those, he remembered reading something about blood trails, and that was what he was looking for.

He didn't find one.

He went back into the unit and opened the door to the day-side. There the light was bright enough to see the floor. It was clean. He checked the logs. The drones weren't scheduled to clean until just before the end of the shift. That, he thought, left only one possibility. He went back inside the unit.

Everyone wore the same style of tight fitting jumpsuit. Each shift, a worker's height, weight and shape were measured and stored, and not just for health reasons. That data was used to ensure that each set of clothes was made with the minimum amount of material. There were no pockets, folds or creases in which a weapon of any kind could be stored. Ely reasoned that if the blade had been in the killer's hand, then a blood trail would have been left in the corridor outside. If he was wrong, then finding camera footage of the killer holding a blade would have the crime solved quickly. But what if the killer hadn't taken the weapon with them?

There were few places within the room for it to be hidden. It couldn't be in the children's pods, they hadn't been opened the night before. The children would have seen it if it was left in the toilet or shower. There hadn't been time to dismantle any of the wall panels, so that left only the obvious; the recycling chute.

There was no space in the Tower for storing personal possessions. Nor was there energy to waste in washing crockery or cleaning clothes. These items, both printed of the same material, were disposed of in a recycling chute. Each hab-unit had one. They would drop down to end up in one of the electro-chemical baths down on Level One, where they would be broken down and reconstituted into fibre-gel, ready to be used again.

The chute was a foot square. Ely pulled on the handle. It was empty, but large enough, he thought, to contain the murder weapon. He tapped out a command.

"Control," he said. "I've stopped the recycling from this hab-unit. Can you confirm?"

"I can confirm you've stopped it for that entire floor."

Ely cursed.

"I just need whatever was thrown out from this unit, last shift."

"You can't isolate it, Ely."

He cursed again.

"Why did you want to stop it?" she asked.

"I think the murder weapon, a blade of some kind, was dropped down the chute."

"That's possible. Hang on." There was a pause. "How big a blade?"

"Between nine and twelve inches, probably with a handle at either end. I don't think it was straight, but possibly curved." He was guessing, and doing so for the benefit of the recording.

"Well, I'm looking at the schematics. Five feet down the chute there are a series of grinders that shred the clothing into one-inch pieces. Four feet below that are a set of rollers that flatten the pieces, then there's another set of grinders after that."

"You're saying the weapon wouldn't fit down there?"

"I think it could fit, I just don't think it could survive. There's no blockage reported. So if it was dropped down there, it's been mulched, just like the clothing."

"And at the bottom? Would any of it be left?"

"Nothing larger than a fibre. Depending on what it was made of, it'll have been recycled, or ended up stuck to the bottom of the vat. If you put in a request to have them emptied, and—"

"No. Forget it. How long does all of that take?"

"To reprocess something? Thirty minutes. At most. If the weapon went down there, it's gone."

He sighed. He wasn't going to empty the vats. It was a task that had to be done by hand, and that would require requisitioning workers from one of the Assemblies. With the loss of a quarter of a million hours already that shift, he knew he wouldn't get the authority to do that.

There was still the question of what, exactly, the weapon had been. The obvious answer was something from one of the Assemblies. He checked the logs. No tools had been reported missing. He tapped out a message, asking the supervisors to manually check, but he stopped himself before sending it. They would want to know the reason for the request. Whatever explanation he gave them, the message he sent would be leaked to the newsfeeds. He didn't think either Councillor Cornwall or the Chancellor would be happy with that.

He checked the time. He was surprised to see that two hours had passed. He had to clear the room for the next shift. That meant he had to get rid of the bodies. That at least, he knew how to do. He called the infirmary.

"What?" Nurse Gower answered.

"I've two bodies here. I need them collected."

"Two bodies? In one shift? How did..." she began, then stopped. "No, don't tell me. I don't care. You need to come up to the infirmary and sentence Grimsby. You do that and we'll come and take care of your bodies."

"No," Ely said, deciding that for once, he'd pull rank. "You come down here and get these bodies. The unit is needed next shift." Because Grimsby did need to be dealt with, he added, "and afterwards, I'll come back up with you to deal with Grimsby. Unless you want four people from the next shift sleeping up in the infirmary."

"We're on our way," she snapped.

Ely took his helmet off and looked at the room just with his eyes. The Greenes had entered, then gone to sleep. Someone had come in and murdered them. Whoever it was hadn't hesitated. Nor had they lingered after the deed was done. The killer hadn't been monitored coming into the room, nor in the corridor outside it. He found himself looking at the camera.

"Control. That camera. When was it moved?"

"One thing at a time, Ely. I'll add that to the list."

"Just give me a—"

"Constable. I've already told you. You'll have to wait." She clicked off.

Ely took one last look around the unit. Something was nagging at the back of his mind, a loose memory of something he'd once read, but he couldn't place exactly what. He was still tugging at the thread of memory when the nurses arrived. They were pushing the same two stretchers they'd brought to the lounge a few hours ago. It seemed like an aeon to Ely.

"You said two bodies?" Bradford, the male nurse asked. "Two natural causes in the same pod? That's got to be a..." The man trailed off as he saw the Greenes' bodies.

"It's murder," Ely said.

"Obviously," Bradford said.

Ely glared at him.

"Well?" the man snapped, unapologetic. "What do you want us to do?"

"Take the bodies away."

"Obviously," he said, again. "I meant after that."

"What's the procedure for murder?" Nurse Gower asked.

Ely wasn't sure there was one.

"Take them to the infirmary," he said. "I have to inform the council. They'll make the decision on what we need to do next."

Together the two nurses manoeuvred the bodies onto the stretchers. Ely removed the visor and two wristboards from the slot at the side of the bed and placed them with the stretcher. They would go into storage, ready to be used by someone else. The City couldn't afford the energy required to make any more.

"And you said that you'd come up and take that man's statement," Gower added, pointedly.

"I will," Ely said, following the two nurses out of the door.

He hesitated briefly in the doorway, again feeling like there was something he'd forgotten. Something important. He stepped out onto the day-side corridor. The door closed, and this time the pods were vacant, the room was empty.

And then Ely remembered. Fingerprints. He swiped his hand down the sensor. It was too late. The room was already being sanitised.

Chapter 2 - The Civic Service
Twenty-one hours before the election

"Well?" Nurse Gower asked. She'd stopped a few yards along the corridor.

"What?" Ely asked, still staring at the door.

"That felon, Grimsby. He's still waiting for you to sentence him."

"Right. I will," Ely said. The nurse opened her mouth to protest. "But like I said, I've got to inform the council first," he finished, quickly.

"Ok," the nurse said grudgingly. She didn't move.

"I'll join you up there in a few minutes. I promise."

Reluctantly, she turned and followed her colleague towards the elevator.

Ely had only said it because he wanted some time to collect his thoughts. He knew he wouldn't find it in the close confines of the elevator with the two aloof nurses and the bodies of the victims. But as he watched the nurses push the stretchers into the lift, he realised that he did, indeed, need to inform the council.

He pulled up the contacts for the office of the Chancellor, but then hesitated. Cornwall was going to win the election, and until he did he was still the Councillor for Tower-One. Ely placed the call.

"This is the Office of Councillor Cornwall," an assistant whose voice Ely recognised but had never met, answered. "How can I help you, Constable Ely?"

"I need to speak to the Councillor."

"Of course. And what does this relate to?"

"A crime."

"I guessed as much. I assume this is in regard to the incident in the lounge earlier today?"

"No," Ely said, bluntly.

"It isn't? Well, what crime are you referring to?"

"I need to inform the Councillor directly."

The assistant's derisive snort jarred through Ely. He was glad that even if the administrator pulled up an image from one of the half-dozen cameras in the hallway, his helmet hid his expression.

"You'll have to do better than that, Constable. It's the middle of the night. Councillor Cornwall is asleep." The council, like the retirees, operated on the outside day/night schedule.

"There's been a murder," Ely said, bluntly.

"A what?"

"Two murders, actually. A double homicide." Ely felt some pride he'd remembered the phrase.

"I see... I..."

"You can check the footage I recorded from inside unit 6-4-17, if you want. Then wake up the Councillor. He *will* want to be informed."

There was a long moment in which he thought the assistant had simply ended the call. Then he heard the Councillor's brusque tones.

"What's this about a murder?" Cornwall demanded.

"Two murders, sir. The Greenes. Husband and wife. They were killed in their pods whilst they slept. That was in Unit 6-4-17."

"Constable, I can understand you are under some considerable strain. That, however, is no reason to forget the correct nomenclature."

"Murdered in their 'beds', sir, in Sea View," Ely corrected himself.

"And you're sure this is murder?" Cornwall asked.

Ely took a breath.

"Sir," he said, "there's camera footage of the bodies. If you check the recordings from my visor you will be able to see for yourself."

"Just a moment." There was a pause before Cornwall spoke again, "I see. And who did it?"

"I... I don't know sir."

"Well, I thought that would be simple enough to find out," Cornwall said. "Who went into the room last night?"

"Just the Greenes."

"I meant other than the Greenes?"

"No one, sir."

"It says here that they have two children. Well, it was probably one of them."

"No sir, I don't think so. I've checked their activity this morning and it seems normal."

"Murderers are not normal, Constable. Would we expect someone who could commit such a heinous crime to be remorseful afterwards?"

"During the shift in question, the door to the unit, I mean the 'home', opened at three a.m., shift time. It opened again three minutes and forty seconds later. During that time both of the children's pods, I mean 'beds', were closed. I really don't think it was either of them."

"Could it have been murder-suicide?" Cornwall asked, but continued before Ely could answer, "No, I suppose not."

"No sir. If it was, the weapon would have still been in the pod." He didn't bother correcting himself this time. "It wasn't there."

"No? Where was it?"

"I..." Ely decided a guess was better than uncertainty. "It was destroyed, sir. In the recycling chute."

"You know this for a fact?"

"No sir, not without absolute certainty. Nor will I without draining out the recycling vats. If you want to authorise that..."

"No, no. We can't have any more disruption. If you think that the weapon has been destroyed, then I'll take your word for it. That is something, though. It suggests that whatever the motive for this vile act, there won't be a repeat of it."

That wasn't what Ely had meant. Before he could think of a way to correcting the Councillor, Cornwall continued, "What else do you know?"

"Their throats were slit."

"I can see that. What else?"

"Well, er... it happened quickly. The killer entered the room, murdered the Greenes, and left again without any hesitation."

"I see. And how does that help you apprehend this felon?"

It didn't.

"I'm following up on a number of leads, sir. The camera was turned to face the wall, and the cameras in the corridor didn't record anyone going in. I'm operating under the assumption that this killer has someway of accessing the records in our system."

There was a sharp intake of breath.

"That's impossible. I was assured that could never happen. I have... I have other calls I must make. Keep me informed, Constable. Keep me informed." The Councillor clicked off.

Ely stared at the blank screen for a moment. He had a question to ask of the Councillor himself. He called the office again, and again the assistant answered.

"Yes? What now?"

"The bodies. What am I to do with them?"

"Bodies? Oh, the Greenes. Hold on. I'll look it up." Ely waited. "I've ordered a transport to take them to Tower-Thirteen," the assistant said. "There will have to be an autopsy."

"And..." Ely began, but the assistant had ended the call.

And what about the children, Ely had been about to ask. He wasn't going to call a third time. He decided it didn't have to be his problem. He tapped out a message, informing their Instructor to break the news to them. He made a note to double check the recording from that conversation. The children's reactions might be interesting. He was certain they weren't involved, but perhaps they knew something.

A light began to flash in the corner of his screen. It was an urgent message from Nurse Gower. She wanted to know why he wasn't in the infirmary or, more importantly, why Grimsby still was.

Unable to put it off any longer, he walked over to the elevator, and headed up to the infirmary.

"You have the right to a trial, your guilt to be judged by a jury of your peers. Should you chose to waive the right to trial, I will issue sentencing here and now. That judgement will be binding, with no possibility of an appeal," Ely said.

"Yeah, I know," Grimsby moaned. He seemed smaller hunched on the small chair in the corner of the infirmary. His arm was now covered in a plastic case.

"Which is it?"

"I'll go with you. Sentencing here and now."

Ely nodded. He glanced down at the screen on his wristboard, to make sure that the cameras in the infirmary had recorded that. The helmet was just too uncomfortable to wear. He'd taken it off the moment he'd finished his call with the Councillor. He tapped out a command.

"That's been notarised and logged. You made the right decision," he added. Grimsby looked up at him. Ely tapped out another command. On a screen on the infirmary wall a list came up with the names of all the citizens in the Tower. Next to each was a number. Ely scrolled down until he reached Grimsby's. Twelve names below, there was a thick red line.

"I see you're on 10,073 points."

"I'm on the ballot for the first colony ship." Defiance flared for a moment, before Grimsby added, in a more subdued tone, "Or I was."

Good, Ely thought, the man understood.

Points were the only currency the City had. They had once been awarded for inter-Tower competitions. A long time ago, before Ely had left school, there had even been competitions between the cities. Sporting, music, arts, anything that could be competed in, was, as long as it could be done virtually. Even then there had been no energy to waste transporting people halfway across the planet or even on frivolous trips to the other Towers. And then there had come the rains and there wasn't the energy or time to waste on the competitions.

But the points had continued even though there were few luxuries on which they could be spent. They were still one of the factors used to determine who was issued a breeding licence, but principally they were used to allocate places on the colony ships.

The first ship only had places for one thousand citizens. Those places were to be determined by a ballot, scheduled to be held shortly after the election. The threshold for entry into that ballot was 10,000 points.

A point could be earned for every extra hour spent in Recreation. That was how most citizens accrued them. Grimsby, Ely noted, was different. He'd earned his through popularity. Every six months, each citizen was given five points that they could award to someone else. Grimsby had procured more than three hundred of his that way.

"You are currently seventy-three points over the threshold. You know the law. I'm meant to dock you one point per hour lost."

"I was just defending myself," Grimsby said "I didn't—"

"I know you didn't throw the first punch. I saw. But I also saw you kick the man when he was down. That kick is the reason he was transported to Tower-Thirteen. One worker's lost labour whilst he recovers works out at two hundred hours, and that's before adding in the energy cost of transportation, the labour of the nurses here, the doctors over on Tower-Thirteen—"

"Hang on, that's not fair," Grimsby protested. "I mean, what are the nurses going to do otherwise. That's what they're here for, isn't it?"

"You think that their time is better spent taking care of you when it could be spent in Recreation or down on one of the Assemblies?" Ely retorted. "And what of the loss to Tower-One. The man won't be sent back here. Most likely he'll be sent to the launch site for his part in the riot."

"But then he'll still be working, won't he? Whether it's here or at the launch site, he'll be productive," Grimsby argued.

"That's not the law. The labour has been lost to Tower-One. And the law says I can fine you one point per hour lost. And that worker has been lost for good."

"What are you saying?" Grimsby whined.

"It's rather poetic," Ely said. "It will take seventeen years and nine months to breed up a replacement for Mr Carlisle. That was what you were fighting about, wasn't it? Breeding up more unproductive mouths. Well, thanks to you, that's what we now need. Those seventeen years and nine months represents nearly fifty thousand hours of labour lost."

"You're fining me for fifty thousand hours?" he stammered in shock.

"I could do. That's what the letter of the law allows." Ely let the words hang there, waiting to see if Grimsby would notice the branch being held out for him. He didn't.

"I'm inclined to be lenient," Ely continued. "Enough labour has been lost to this Tower today already." Ely glanced at the two bodies lying on the stretchers in the middle of the room. Grimsby didn't follow his gaze. The man was so lost in his own wretchedness, he hadn't even noticed them. "I'm docking you seventy-two points," Ely went on, "The rest I'm holding back. One more infraction and I'll charge you immediately. You won't make it onto any of the colony ships. You'll be left here on Earth. Do you understand?"

"Yes. Thank you, thank you. They always said you civic servants were..."

Ely waved him into silence. He was about to send him away, then he remembered that he'd allocated the man's 'home' to one of the Durhams for the night. He glanced over at Nurse Gower. He'd never got on with the nurses. Or to be more accurate they, who had been working in the civic service long before he was appointed, didn't get on with him.

He picked up his helmet and stood up.

"You can stay here for the rest of this shift. Try and get some sleep without one of the machines. Consider that..." he glanced at Nurse Gower, "... an extra punishment."

He headed out the door.

Chapter 3 - Control
Twenty hours before the election

"How could you not have noticed the camera was pointing at the wall?" Ely asked.

"Because it's just me down here to watch 12,000 citizens," Vauxhall said.

"I know that there's just you here." The other two Controllers had been re-assigned at the same time as the other Constables. "But I thought the video feeds were sent to Tower-Thirteen. I thought that was the whole point of having the cameras; that the prisoners on a short sentence went through the footage."

"Ely," she said with puzzled patience, "there aren't any short sentences. Not for the last three years. Didn't you know?"

"What? In the last year alone, I've sentenced seven people to three months or less."

"No, Ely. You recommended that. Your judgement is only a recommendation. No one gets three months."

"That's..." he stopped himself. He was going to say that it was criminal, but that was sedition, even if said by him. He glanced over to where he'd left his helmet. There were no cameras in the Control Room and the helmet, in the absence of an iris to scan, would have switched itself off. Nevertheless, Arthur had taught him to always be cautious. "...that's something I didn't realise," he finished.

"When was the last time you came in here?" Vauxhall asked.

"Last month?"

"It was last year," she said.

"Really? It's the patrols and the Recreation and, well, there's just so much to do," he said weakly.

"Right. Exactly. Which is why, when the worst crime we usually have to deal with is some stupid fight over nothing, it would be utterly redundant to have useful workers spending precious hours just going through camera footage."

"So what happens to the felons? Where are they?"

"They go to the launch site. Don't get me wrong," she added hurriedly. "They're all volunteers. They're given a choice, their sentence will be commuted, and they can go back on the ballot for the ships."

"I knew the sentences were just a recommendation, that it was down to the authorities in Tower-Thirteen to ratify it, I just... I mean, someone should have... I..."

"Look, if it makes you feel better, I only found out by accident," Vauxhall said, taking pity on the younger man. "Most of what I know I've found out that way. I don't think this is something that's exactly hidden from us, but it's not the kind of thing they want going public. I mean, it's basically saying that if you commit a crime, no matter how severe, you'll be sent to work outside where the only real punishment is having to wear thick protective clothing in case the wind changes to blow in from the north. And despite the clothing, the altitude, the heat and all the rest, imagine being able to work outside. So no, it's not a surprise this one was kept hidden from us." She leant forwards. "The real question, though, the one I can't work out, is why they suddenly needed all the extra personnel down there. What changed?" She let the question hang there for a moment before she leant back and went on. "But as I said, that's something I can't work out. Anyway, it wouldn't matter even if there had been a couple of other people watching. Here."

Against two of the four walls were rows of screens. She tapped out a command. The giant pictures of the victims that had been filling the displays were replaced by hundreds of far smaller images.

"There are 12,029 workers in this Tower, right? Let's just forget about the other Towers and the work I end up having to do for them. 12,029 workers, two thirds of whom could be awake at any one time. That's 7,184 visor-mounted cameras I've got to look at." The images on the screen changed. "Now factor in the cameras in the Assemblies, the Twilight Room, the 'farms' and all the corridors in between." The images on the screen changed again. "That's 15,901 cameras for me to watch, assuming I'm not doing something else, such as..." The images changed again, and this time Vauxhall pointed to one, "... guiding in a transport."

Ely peered at the screen.

"Where's that? It's all dark."

"That's the transport pad. It's night outside. Even when it isn't, I've got to guide the transport in through driving rain and 100 mile per hour winds."

"But you can't see anything."

"There are lights," she said, exasperation dripping from her voice, "I'm not turning them on now, that would be wasteful. My point is that it usually takes an hour to bring one in, load and unload it, and send it off again, and for all that time I've got to be focusing on the transport and nothing else. We've got the daily shipment of new components for the Assemblies and the dispatch of the components that have been checked. Then there's the food to be sent to the launch site, and on top of that there's the traffic to Tower-Thirteen. And for each I've got to work out flight trajectories and—"

"Ok, I get it," Ely said, raising his hands in surrender. "There's just you and you're overworked. You don't have time to notice that one camera in one unit isn't pointing the right way. But isn't there some algorithm you could use? Some way of getting the system to find out if a camera is off-centre or something."

"Right, like I didn't think of that. Here." She tapped out another command.

"None of those screens are blank," Ely said.

"No, but each of them has been knocked 'off-centre', as you put it. Most of the time it's done by one of the cleaning drones, and most of the time it's only by a few millimetres."

"A few what?" he asked.

"Less than a fraction of an inch. It's an old form of measurement. It's not important. Then there are these." She tapped out another command, the screens changed. "The fixed-position cameras. Each of these has a scratched casing or a damaged lens. You see, someone has to go through and find the cameras that aren't focusing correctly, that *someone* has to record them and then put in a request for a repair and a replacement. I've been doing that, as often as I can, but do you honestly think that will be approved now, this close to the launch? What would be the point? What, really, is there for the cameras to see?"

"Up until now."

"Right, yes. I know, I know. Look, Ely, there just aren't the resources to spare." She gestured to a mattress held above the floor on a plastic frame. "I don't use the machines. I sleep here now, so I'm only a few seconds away from the screens."

"Fine. I get it." Ely stared at the array of images. "But surely, even if we don't have an image of the killer inside the room, we must have an image from one of the cameras in the corridor. I thought that every inch of the Tower is meant to be recorded."

"Almost every inch. Almost," she admitted.

"What do you mean?"

"Ok, I'll start with the good news. This was the last time the camera was facing into the room." She tapped out a command. The image of a family jostling for position as they got into bed filled the central screens.

"Who are they?" Ely asked.

"Just watch. There. They're all in bed. Now I need to fast forward...to... here. There, see." The camera slowly swivelled to face the wall.

"When was that?"

"Two weeks ago."

"Someone went into the room to move the camera, but then waited two weeks before they took advantage of it. How many shifts is that?"

"Two hundred and eighty-seven. It's not exactly two weeks, but the point still stands."

"That has to be the killer."

"It has to be, yes," Vauxhall said. "But think of it this way, two hundred and eighty-six sets of families slept in that unit before the Greenes were murdered."

"And were there any useful images from the corridor outside on the night the camera was moved?"

"No, Ely, that's what I meant when I said nearly every inch was covered. Look." The image changed again. "We know that the door on the night-side opened, both when the camera was moved and when the Greenes were murdered. Right?"

"Right."

"So what do you see?" she asked.

He stared at the screen. There was a section of hallway with a series of doors leading of it. Then he realised it wasn't what he could see, but what he couldn't.

"You can't see the door to that unit," he said.

"Exactly. Here, this is the next camera along." She tapped a command and the image changed, showing a slightly different angle of the same stretch of hallway.

"You still can't see the door."

"The corridor curves. Add that to the support strut there, and the view of the door is blocked."

"Well, what about one of the other cameras?"

"I've checked. None of them can see the door to that unit."

"How is that... no, it doesn't matter. To open that door the killer had to walk along the corridor, there has to be a picture of them."

"No, Ely, that's what I'm telling you." Her fingers moved. The screen split. "These are all the cameras along the corridor, in both directions. This is just after shift-change. You see, there? That's the Greenes. Now watch."

The corridor filled with people and, one at a time, they drifted into their unit for their shift's sleep.

"This will save some time if I just speed it up." She began tapping out another command.

"It would save even more if you just told me."

"Sorry. Ok, basically no one went along that corridor until the next shift-change. No. Sorry, no, what I meant to say is that no one is *recorded* going along that corridor."

"You mean this is a ghost?" Ely asked without trying to hide the scorn in his voice.

"You mean do I think this is the descendent of someone who got stuck outside after the Towers were sealed and somehow managed to survive down in the tunnels? No, of course not, that's just a story. Besides, the tunnels are flooded. What I meant was that I've been looking at it, over and over again, and I think you can get down that corridor, all the way to the door to that unit, without being recorded by any of the cameras."

"But we'd still have a record of their position in the Tower."

"Not if they went off-net. That's what I'm trying to tell you. We don't monitor the people, we're monitoring the wristboards. That's how we know where everyone is, what their heart rate is, when they ate, when they're at work. When they sleep, the pods take over. But if they take the wristboard off, the system doesn't know where they are."

"So, to become invisible, all you would have to do is take off your wristboard?"

"Well, yes and no. I mean, the cameras would still record that part of the corridor. So you'd have to know where they were and, for instance, that these two here..." she pointed, "... rotate, and you'd want to know the timing, but you could watch it and learn."

"And you knew about these blind spots?" Ely asked, failing to hide the accusation in his voice.

"Well, I knew there were some, sure. But I didn't know there were so many. I mean, no one could, not unless you went through the schematics and crossed off every inch of corridor against an image."

"Or if you stood in a corridor," Ely said, "and looked up, saw the camera move and realised that you were no longer being recorded. It would take years of planning."

"Even then you'd have to have access to the system."

"Which we know the killer did, don't we? No alarms went off."

"That's a different part of the system."

"If our killer had access to one part, then why couldn't they have access to all of it?"

"Because they moved the camera. So we know they don't have access to everything, we just don't know how much."

"Right." Ely felt a flush of embarrassment that he hadn't realised that himself.

"So let me get this straight. They can access the alarms and turn those off, they can open the doors, but they can't erase the camera footage?"

"That's what it looks like."

"And there are, what, two hundred and fifty families in that shift eligible to use that room?"

"Two hundred and sixty-seven."

"So, statistically speaking, the killer, having moved the camera, wouldn't have to wait more than ninety days for any one family to use that room."

"Yes, they're allocated randomly to ensure no one develops any attachment to them."

"Interesting. And it's been fourteen days. Maybe this had nothing to do with the Greenes then. Maybe..." he didn't finish the thought. It was to terrifying to say out loud.

"What?" Vauxhall asked

"Well, what if the Greenes weren't specifically targeted. What if it was just about disrupting production?"

"You mean sabotage? Why?"

"I don't know," Ely said.

"Well, where do we go from here?"

"There's something I read once." It was one of the few things he could remember from the forensics textbooks. "Absence of evidence is evidence itself. So the killer can turn off the alarms, they can hide from the cameras, they can make it seem as if they weren't in that corridor, but..." and Ely smiled as he realised he was right, "...they can't hide their presence from the system."

"You mean the wristboard data? I told you that no one was recorded using that corridor during the time of the murder."

"Yes. And that means someone took it off. They had to have left it somewhere. But that means that for the time the murder took place, the killer went off-net. We believe the murder happened at three a.m., that's the middle of a shift. Can you think of any reason at all for anyone in the Tower to take their wristboard off at that time? Well, can you?"

"No, none at all."

"So," he said, "instead of looking to see where they were, just look for who wasn't anywhere. Do you see?"

"Ok," Vauxhall said, slowly as she returned to the screens. "That makes sense. Hang on."

"How long will this take?" Ely asked.

"I said hang on... here." A list came up on the screen.

"Who are they?" he asked.

"That's all the people who were off-net during the time of the murder."

"All of them? But there are so many."

"There are forty-seven people," she said.

"No," Ely said. "Forty-seven suspects."

He picked up his helmet.

"Where are you going?" Vauxhall asked.

"To interrogate them," he said simply, as he walked out of the door.

He'd made it twenty paces before an alert came up on his display. He had an incoming call from Chancellor Stirling. Bracing himself, he answered it.

"Murders, Constable. Murders! Why didn't you inform me directly?" the Chancellor demanded.

"Ma'am, I was waiting until I had something to report."

"You don't think this ruinous loss of production was something worth reporting? Do you know how much labour has been lost?"

"About a quarter of a million hours ma'am."

"Our current estimates," a man answered, "put it at three hundred thousand. It is likely to be far higher."

Ely knew that voice as well. It belonged to Councillor Henley, the man Stirling wanted to take control of Tower-One. He was expected to win. His opponent, Chester from Tower-Five, had made some ill-advised comments about population increase ten years ago. There was no doubt as to who had leaked the recordings of them to the newsfeeds. There were no candidates from Tower-One standing. The Assemblies had a long tradition of not wasting workers on something so frivolous as politics.

"Three hundred thousand hours lost, all from Tower-One," Henley said. "What do you have to say about that?"

That it was a matter for Councillor Cornwall, Ely thought. But he didn't say it.

"As I said, I wanted to make some progress with the investigation before reporting in."

"Well get on with it," Stirling snapped. "Why were the Greenes killed?"

"I don't know ma'am, but," Ely added quickly, "I believe it was sabotage."

"Sabotage?" There was a sharp intake of breath from the Chancellor.

"Are you sure?" Henley asked.

"I won't be certain until I've made an arrest, but at this point that seems the most likely motive."

"I see," the Chancellor said. "You mean it's a guess. And you are also telling us that you've not made an arrest. Do you know who the killer is?"

"No ma'am. Not definitively. But I do have suspects."

"Suspects, plural?" Henley asked.

"Yes sir."

"Well, spit it out, man. Who are they?"

"I've established that the killer had to be someone from within Tower-One, and have eliminated all but forty-seven names from that list."

"Forty-seven? You're not saying they were all involved?" Henley asked.

"No sir," Ely said, though now he wondered whether there might be more than one person involved. "I believe the crime was committed by just one individual."

"And how do you want to proceed from here?" Chancellor Stirling asked.

"I was planning on interrogating them all," Ely said.

"No," Henley said curtly. "That would be too great a disruption and we can't afford any more of those. Not now that..."

The Chancellor cleared her throat pointedly. Henley didn't finish his sentence.

"It would only take an hour or two per suspect," Ely said, to fill the loaded silence.

"I imagine it will take a lot longer than that," Henley said. "And the election is only a matter of hours away."

"But Chancellor—" Ely began to protest.

"No," she interrupted. "Henley is correct. We must minimize all disruption. You say you've identified forty-seven suspects. If you say they are not all involved, then you must work harder. I will allow you to interview five. No more. In the meantime, I'm ordering all transportation from Tower-One suspended. If we can do nothing else, we can ensure that this killer remains your problem."

"And, Constable," Henley said, "when you do catch this killer, remember that there is only one sentence possible. This killer is of no use to our society. There is no possibility of rehabilitation. The killer must die. When you find him, throw him out of the airlock. We will not waste the energy transporting him here. If you manage this, though I doubt you will, perhaps it will go someway to mitigating the damage your failures have caused."

"Yes," Stirling said, "I concur. Execute this killer. Justice should be swift, Constable. We've seen your logs. Too often you skulk in the shadows. The fault here lies with you. Were you a more visible presence, were you feared, then this crime would not have occurred. Nor, had you been in the lounge, would that fight have begun. All these wasted hours can be firmly placed at your feet, Constable. I will remind you, again, that the election has not yet happened. I am in power. If you are unable to perform your duties, you will be removed and replaced. I hope I make myself clear. Productivity must be maintained."

The Chancellor clicked off.

Ely stared into space for a moment. He couldn't believe it. He'd always suspected that Henley was the power behind the throne, but he'd not realised quite how influential the man was until now.

They were going to make him the scapegoat. It wouldn't work. Rather, it wouldn't be enough to secure Stirling victory in the polls. That was scant comfort. If Ely was dismissed, he would be sent to the launch site. He didn't want that. It wasn't the harsh conditions that worried him, but an ignominious dismissal would spell the end of his hopes to one day stand for election himself.

Ely brought up the list of suspects on his display and began to sort through them as he headed towards the elevator. He needed somewhere quiet to work, but the Chancellor was right in one respect, she was still in charge. He still had to obey her, which meant he had to be seen. He headed up to the lounge.

Chapter 4 - Children
Eighteen hours before the election

"In under two years we'll be on Mars," one said.

"No, in under two years the first of us is going to be on Mars," another replied.

"It's the same difference. We'll be on Mars, and The People's City will just be leaving Earth's orbit, and The City of Rights, well, they'll be still stuck here on Earth."

"Yeah, but what I'm trying to say, is that it doesn't matter which of us gets there first. What counts, what'll matter to history, is who gets all their population transplanted there first."

"Oh come on," the first one replied, "In a century's time does it matter who was on Earth last? No, of course not. People are only ever going to remember which nation got to Mars first."

"There," a woman said. "You just said it yourself. First or last, what counts is that there are people who'll remember. No, no, think about it, I mean really think about it. What matters more, getting to Mars or being the people who write the history?"

"You're saying," another said, "that it doesn't matter what we do, just what we say we do? Doesn't the truth matter to you? What does it mean to be British if we aren't honest with our descendants?"

Ely cleared his throat loudly, but he didn't look up. He was trying to be considerate. Debates were allowed, they were encouraged, but this one was straying dangerously close to sedition. Without any audio recordings to analyse and process, the only evidence that this was anything other than a spirited conversation were the increased heart rates and elevated blood pressures. By law, those themselves weren't enough to press any charges. But if he looked up, then his camera would register the individuals concerned, and he would be expected to file a report. He really didn't want any more paperwork, so he kept his head down as he went over the schematics of the corridor outside Unit 6-4-17. He was trying to be considerate, but the group in the centre of the lounge weren't making it easy.

"I, uh, I didn't mean it like that," the woman said. "What I meant was that unless we can establish a thriving colony then it won't matter whether we were first, second, or third. If the colony fails, then there won't be any more history. Britain will die. Do you see?"

Ely heard a shuffling of feet. Either no one did get the woman's point or they were reluctant to agree with her whilst he was sitting so close by.

"The point I'm making," she went on, "is that we need to focus on production, not on speed. I'm trying to say it's not a race."

"Oh? And what about civic pride?" Ely recognised that as one of the voices from earlier. He wished he had a way of blocking out sounds.

"Yes, yes, that's important," she said hurriedly. "Of course that's important, but we can be proud of a good job done. We can be proud of our own work without constantly comparing it to the other two cities."

"What she's saying," someone else added, a snide tone to her voice, "is that she wants more children."

"Oh? Is that it?" the man asked.

"Well, maybe, but..."

There was a collective snort from most of the crowd, as if they were finally getting to the root of the debate.

"You see, that's the problem. You talk about Production First, but you don't really know what it means. More children on Earth means more people to take to Mars. That means more trips and that means more energy, which means more people. It would be a never ending cycle, don't you see?"

"Without children, there won't be a future," she replied.

"Oh, I'm not against children," the man said expansively. "I'm just saying there's a time and a place for 'em. Once we're on Mars, then fine, we can have as many as the society can support. But now? Can we really support any more unproductive mouths? Well, can we?"

Ely thought he felt the eyes of the crowd glance over at him. That, he had long ago decided, was the problem with the Chancellor's decree that he be seen. It was a constant reminder that the labour of others was being expended to keep him fed. Up until now, there had been little enough crime that he sometimes agreed with the statement.

Ordinarily, the table in the corner of the lounge was a good place to work. Usually after work and Recreation, workers spent their few off-shift hours lost in the worlds behind their displays. When people did talk it was usually quietly, and these days usually about what life might be like on Mars. But not this shift.

Ely wasn't sure whether it was Councillor Cornwall, the Greene children's Instructor, or the Chancellor herself who had leaked the news about the murders. It didn't matter, it was Cornwall who'd managed to capitalise on the event first. He had issued a statement clarifying the rumours, and that had begun the debate.

"A terrible event has befallen us," Cornwall had said, "Two highly productive workers have been taken from us. They have been killed. This was not natural causes, nor was it an accident. They were murdered. Make no mistake, this madman will be caught. When he is, he will face the only justice appropriate to such a heinous crime. But we must not let this distract us from the great work ahead of us. We must not lose focus. We must continue, together, to strive for our future, our children's future, and the future of our City, our Britain."

Ely knew, well enough, that Cornwall had only wanted to get the statement out before Stirling and Henley. Nonetheless, he felt a small sense of betrayal that he had not been informed first. And who had said the killer was a man?

What had really surprised Ely was the response from the citizenry. The newsfeeds were already full of articles, written mostly by off-duty workers from the other Towers. They all focused on the implications of lost labour, and had turned the debate to that of productivity. Ely had thought that the workers in Tower-One, being closer to the crime and its inherent threat, would have responded differently, yet they too seemed more concerned with the debate on population increase than the immediate danger.

Ely tried, once more, to concentrate on the schematics.

"What if we were to reduce the school leaving age?" The woman's voice broke through Ely's concentration. "Councillor Cornwall has hinted he's going to consider it when he's Chancellor."

"If. If he's elected," someone else said. There was a general laugh at that.

"That's missing the point..." The man began to repeat, and misquote, a speech that Cornwall had given a few days before.

Ely ignored him. He'd just had an idea.

He had started by reasoning that the killer must have known the Greenes. He refused to believe, and hoped he was right, that the killer had chosen them randomly. So he had begun by getting the system to identify which of the forty-seven suspects had had any contact with the victims. What he'd quickly discovered was that, since the Greenes were on the same shift as the suspects, each of them had come into contact with the victims dozens of times each week.

It was after that, when he was beginning to doubt he would find any evidence before the Chancellor decided to throw him to the wolves, that the idea came to him.

All he had to do was check the schematics, and see which of the suspects could actually get from their pod to the victims unit, and back, within the time they were off-net.

Out of the forty-seven suspects, Silas Glastonbury had spent the shortest time off-net. Unlike the Greenes, he was single and had spent the shift in question in a unit on the level below. According to the same record, he had been off-net from 02:58:45 to 03:04:18.

Ely had looked again at the schematics and decided that whilst it was theoretically possible for the man to have made it to Unit 6-4-17 and back in under five and a half minutes, it was unlikely. Certainly it was unlikely that anyone could do it whilst being so careful that they weren't caught on camera. Which meant Glastonbury was almost definitely not the killer. At the same time, it was too much of a coincidence for the man not to be somehow involved. Interrogating him should lead to an explanation of what the other forty-six were doing and thus eliminate most of them from his enquiries. At the very least, it would give the impression of action. He stood up and left the lounge.

As he rode the elevator up to the Assembly he checked the time. It was only ten minutes until shift-change. He considered waiting and arresting Glastonbury more quietly. He dismissed the idea almost instantly. He wanted the citizenry to think he was doing something, and more than that, he wanted to wreak a small piece of revenge upon Chancellor Stirling. Glastonbury was one of Stirling's few registered supporters in Tower-One. Arresting him publicly would be the price the Chancellor would pay for her disdain.

Ely checked the feed from the camera on Glastonbury's visor. The man sat in front of a section of conveyor belt no different than any of the hundreds of others in the Tower. To his left a panel lifted and a piece of circuitry moved along the belt to stop in front of him. In Glastonbury's right hand was a sensor. He moved it down to touch a section of wiring. A light in front of him turned green. With his left hand he pressed a button. The conveyor belt moved, taking the approved circuitry off, and bringing a new piece in its place.

It seemed nearly identical to the same dull work that Ely remembered doing himself during his brief time in the Assemblies. It was monotonous, it was repetitive, and it was utterly vital. There would be no way of replacing, nor repairing, a faulty component once the ships were launched. It was why a place on the first ship was so coveted. With each successive journey the ships made, the risk of some catastrophic failure increased.

The elevator stopped.

As Ely walked along the corridor towards the Assembly in which Glastonbury worked, he brought up the records for the other workers. There were two teams of six with one supervisor. Discounting the suspect, and a worker who didn't wear one, that left eleven people with visors to record and upload the arrest. Fortuitously, Ely saw that one of those workers had the fifth most popular newsfeed in the City. Ely smiled. Everyone would know about the arrest before the next shift had begun.

He hesitated at the door and brought up the view from the cameras inside. The citizens were still working. He waited.

A few minutes later an alarm sounded, and the conveyor belts rolled forwards empty. The shift had finished. One by one, the workers began to stand up. Ely overrode the clean room protocols - with the components all sealed away and the drones about to sanitise the room it wouldn't matter - and opened the door.

"Silas Glastonbury," he said, imbuing his voice with all the menace he could muster. All heads turned to stare at him. Ely was gratified to see the small red lights on the visors come on. They were recording. "Glastonbury," Ely said again as he walked into the low ceilinged room, "You're under arrest."

And now some of the lights turned green, indicating they were uploading live.

Glastonbury stood frozen in place.

"Put your hands on your head," Ely said, more quietly now that he had the entire room's attention.

"I'm... But my work. It's vital," Glastonbury stammered.

"All work is vital. That is why I waited until the shift was over," Ely said. He could see fear in the man's eyes and he recognised it as the fear of a guilty man, caught.

"I... but... I..." The man stammered, and he started to back away from the Constable.

Ely had had enough. He grabbed the man's right arm, twisted it up and behind his back.

"Go on, I've questions you need to answer," he said, pushing the man towards the door. Conscious of the cameras, he didn't do it gently.

"What are the charges?" a woman asked. According to Ely's display she was the Assembly overseer.

"This is in relation to the murder of Alphonse and Finnya Greene," Ely said, loudly. The supervisor backed away.

Ely frogmarched Glastonbury out of the Assembly. It was only when he was in the corridor that he realised his mistake. He'd nowhere to question the suspect. The last time, the only time, that he had conducted an interview had been shortly after he'd begun his career as a Constable.

That had been a matter of sedition based on evidence recorded on the other-net. Of course, Ely couldn't let the agitator know that the other-net was constantly monitored. He hadn't known himself until Arthur had told him.

The interview itself had taken place down on Level Two in the small cell that they'd then had. Ely remembered the experience well. It had taken a whole shift to break her, but he had, and then sentenced her to 10,000 hours on one of the penal gangs. That had been his first proper case.

And then, almost a year later, there had been the Re-Organisation, and the small office, and the smaller cell, had been re-allocated. Up until now, that hadn't mattered. He thought quickly.

"Don't move," he snarled, pushing the suspect against the wall.

He tapped out a command onto his wristboard, commandeering an elevator. That would get him into trouble, he knew, but he couldn't see an alternative. As an afterthought, and as he waited for it, he tapped out a message to all the workers who were queuing for it below. It simply said 'requisitioned for use in the interrogation of a suspect in the murder of Finnya and Alphonse Greene'. That, he thought, would add to the public interest, keep the story rolling, and help him keep his job. The elevator arrived. He shoved Glastonbury in, then tapped out a command to take them up.

"Where are we going?" Glastonbury asked. The red light on his visor was blinking. Ely accessed his account and turned the man's camera off.

"Level Seventy-Seven."

"To see the Councillor?" If the man had sounded scared before, now he sounded terrified.

"No. You're not worth Councillor Cornwall's time. I'm taking you outside."

"What? But no one can survive out there. We'll die."

"Not we. You."

"But I haven't done anything." It was a weak protest.

"That's it. Keep lying. It won't matter. I have my orders. There's been too much disruption." The elevator doors opened. Ely pushed

Glastonbury out in front of him. "Deducting points won't work. Not anymore. An example needs to be made. Of you."

The man continued stammering out a protest as Ely pushed him down the hallway and towards the airlock that led to the transport pad. He stopped at the end of the corridor.

"Through there is the outside," Ely said, pointing at the grey metal doors of the airlock. "Rain so heavy you won't be able to breathe, wind so strong you'll be blown up, and off, and over twenty miles before you hit the ground." Everyone knew what life was like outside.

"Please..." the man whimpered.

"Unless," Ely said, then paused, waiting for the dim prospect of hope to take hold.

"Unless what?"

"State your name."

"What? You know my name."

"For the record," Ely said. Unlike the workers, his cameras were always recording and had no light to indicate as such.

"Record? Silus Glastonbury."

"Age."

"But..."

"Age?"

"Thirty-nine."

"Occupation?"

"I work in the Assemblies. You know that."

"Yes," Ely said. "And those were the easy questions. Did you kill Mr and Mrs Greene?"

"What? No. Of course not."

"When did you first meet them?"

"I didn't, I mean, I've never met..."

"Really. What's this?" Ely tapped out a command. An image came up on Glastonbury's display showing him sitting at a table in one of the lounges next to Mrs Greene. "And this one," Ely tapped out another command. The image changed to a video from the Recreation Room. The two Greenes were pedalling away just like the hundreds of others. To the left of the two victims were their children. To the right was Glastonbury.

"I mean, but that's..." Glastonbury took a breath. "So we work the same shift. So do four thousand others. I mean, I was bound to be standing by them, or sitting next to them, or something at some point."

"So you do know who they are. Why did you lie?"

"What?"

"A moment ago. You said you'd never met them, now you admit you had."

"I didn't..." Glastonbury took a breath. "I didn't know they were the two who died. I saw some rumours during the break, but I've been on shift, haven't I? I haven't had a chance to read any articles or anything."

"And you admit now you've met them before."

"No, I meant I knew that they worked here, of course I did. I didn't know their names. I just knew their faces. I mean, I know what dozens of people look like—"

"And they're your next victims are they? That's your plan is it? You stalk the corridors and seek out good, diligent workers. Why do you do it? Why do you kill?"

"It's not me. I didn't do it. I've never done anything."

"You're lying." Ely grabbed his arm and shoved him a few feet closer to the airlock. "I don't have time for this. If you're not going to answer truthfully, I'm not going to bother asking any more questions."

"But I am, I'm innocent. I haven't done anything wrong. I didn't kill them."

"But you know who did," Ely said.

"How could I?"

Ely slammed the man against the wall, hard.

"Where were you when they were killed?"

"It happened last shift, didn't it? I was asleep."

"Really?"

"Yes."

"This is your final chance," Ely said. "The next lie will be your last." He tapped out a command. Glastonbury's face screwed up as he focused on the string of data that had just appeared on his display.

"I don't know what any of that..."

"For five and a half minutes last night you went off-net. At the same time, the Greenes were murdered. Either you killed the Greenes or you know who did."

"I don't."

"You were asleep. You woke up. You got out of your pod. You didn't put your wristboard on."

"I... there's... there's no law about waking up."

"No, you're right, there's not. Nor is there a law that says you have to wear a wristboard at all times. But you went off-net at the same time as the Greenes were murdered. Do you have another explanation?" He paused a moment and saw the hesitation in the man's face. "No? Fine. The charge is sabotage." He began to drag the suspect the last few yards to the airlock.

"No. Stop. You can't."

"I can. I have my orders. No trial, just the execution. No more wasted hours. I'm sick of people like you. Everyone else is able to sacrifice and strive in order for there to be a future for the human race, but you..." He slammed Glastonbury into the metal door of the airlock. "... You think you're above the law. No, I'm not going to have any more of it."

The man started to cry.

Ely moved over to the panel to the side of the door.

"Silus Glastonbury, for wilful complicity in sabotage, I sentence you to —"

"No, wait. Please. I'll tell you. It's the water." The words came out so quickly they were barely coherent. "There's a way to get more. The system doesn't work, not properly. Everyone knows."

"Stop," Ely said firmly. "Start again. Slowly."

"The water for the showers. The hot water. Everyone gets one issue of three minutes per day. The system resets itself at three a.m., once a day. I mean, once every twenty-four hours, when it's three a.m. for our shift. It's meant to do it just at shift-change, but from three a.m., for half an hour, you can have another shower and that's not logged."

Ely stared at the man, disbelieving.

"Hot water? You force yourself to wake up in the middle of the night just to have an extra shower?"

"Yes! That's what I'm telling you."

"Shut up."

Ely pulled up the records for water usage for the Tower. He checked the figures for three a.m. There was a discrepancy.

"Control?"

"Yes, Constable."

"Did you hear that?"

"Oh yes. I've been watching since you arrested him. You should have warned me."

"Can you confirm what he said?"

"Yes. I think so. Give me a moment. Yes, there's an increased water usage during that time."

Ely turned his attention back to Glastonbury.

"You said everyone knows. Who's everyone?"

"Everyone. I mean," he added, hurriedly, "it's just one of those things that people know. Like how the purple flavour has more sugar or how the eighth row of machines in the Recreation Room are slightly easier than the rest."

Ely stared at him. He knew about the purple flavouring and the eighth row in the Recreation Room, but he also knew that those were rumours with no more truth to them than the ones about ghosts. The glitch with the hot water, however, that clearly wasn't a rumour, nor was it something that he had ever heard or read before. If it was known and discussed, it wasn't done online, not even on the other-net. That was a chilling thought. He wondered what other conspiracies were taking place without his knowledge.

"I swear, that's all it was," Glastonbury babbled. "I just wanted a hot shower. I didn't have anything to do with the murders."

"How long has this been going on?" Ely asked quietly.

"A year," Glastonbury whispered back. "But I wasn't greedy. I only spent three minutes in there."

"A year. Three minutes a day, three hundred and sixty-five shifts." Multiply that by forty-seven, though Ely wasn't going to tell the felon how many others had done the same as him, "Do you know how much energy you've wasted? We can't afford to waste a single joule. Everyone knows that, everyone except you of course."

"What are you going to do to me?" Glastonbury asked, "It's not sabotage. Not really."

Glastonbury was wrong. It was sabotage, but it wasn't murder. Production had to come first, and Ely doubted that either Councillor Cornwall or Chancellor Stirling would allow him to deport Glastonbury. If they did it for one, they would have to do it for the other forty-six.

"I'm deferring sentence until a full assessment has been conducted into how much damage your greed has done."

Ely grabbed the man's arm and hauled him back to the elevator. He pushed him inside and sent him down to the Recreation Room.

When the doors closed, Ely leant up against the wall and breathed out. It was a serious offence. Had it not been for the murder, it would have been the most serious crime he had ever discovered.

"Control?"

"Ely?"

"Can you look at the other forty-six suspects? Check the water usage for them and—"

"And see if they were doing the same as him. I've already done it. They were."

"Thank you," Ely said.

"What do you want me to do next?"

"Just... I'll be in touch." He clicked off.

He had no suspects in the murder. No leads left at all.

He saw that there were a dozen blinking lights at the bottom of his display. They must have been there for some time, but he'd not noticed them. Most came from various contributors to the newsfeeds, and most of those came from Tower-One. He tapped out a short reply; Glastonbury had been questioned in connection with the murders. The investigation was on-going. More suspects would be questioned shortly.

He hesitated before sending it. The message seemed inadequate, it implied his uncertainty, yet he could think of nothing else he could say. He sent it and blocked all future messages asking for information. Only then did he remember that he should have informed Chancellor Stirling first. He tapped out a slightly longer, but no less vague, message to her.

He looked down the corridor. To the left was Councillor Cornwall's office. Ely had never been inside. He was tempted to ask to speak to the man. Perhaps the politician would have some advice. No, Ely thought, today he would only be concerned with the election.

He sent the same message to the Councillor and headed back to the elevator. He did need advice, and there was only one person who could give it - his former supervisor, Arthur.

Chapter 5 - Retirement
Sixteen hours before the election

"You should have come to me as soon as it happened, my boy," Arthur said, reproachfully.

"There's hardly been time, and I didn't want to bother you," Ely mumbled. Arthur always made him feel like the seventeen-year old he'd been when he was recruited five years ago.

"You mean you wanted to prove you could handle it on your own. I understand lad, and you wouldn't be bothering me. Do you know how dull it gets up here?" The old man gestured at the doors behind him. "All that lot ever want to talk about is the past. It's like they're already dead. No, any distraction is welcome. Well, there's no point talking out here, come on in."

Taking Ely's arm with one hand, he waved his other by the sensor. The doors opened.

Up until the rains began fifteen years ago, the whole of Level Seventy-Six had been given over to the retirees. When the solar panels became useless, the museum was moved out of Level Nine - that space became the Recreation Room. Level Seventy-Six was split in two and most of the older residents of the Twilight Room had moved to Tower-Thirteen. The smaller half of the level became the new museum, though the rarely visited artefacts were so crammed together that the space would be better described as a storeroom. The larger half of Level Seventy-Six was still occupied by the retirees, but with the increased urgency to establish a working colony on Mars, most of the space was given over to row after row of earth-filled allotments.

Tending these was the retirees' continued sacrifice to the good of the Tower. Some were open to the room's atmosphere, others were enclosed in opaque plastic panelling. A mess of wires and pipes snaked into those simulating, as far as possible, the conditions the settlers would find on Mars.

Some plants arrived as sprouting shoots, others as seeds, and all came from frozen storage in Tower-Thirteen. It was one more vital part of the plan to establish a thriving colony; after terraforming, would anything from Earth grow on the red planet?

The rewards for those who volunteered to eschew the luxuries of retirement in Tower-Thirteen were privacy and respect. The City had nothing else to offer them. Yet, with fifty-three 'residents', the Twilight Room was nearly at full occupancy. Though they were allowed to visit the lounges lower down the Tower, they rarely did. It was just as permissible, as long as an appointment was made forty-eight hours in advance, for workers to visit their aged relatives, but that was equally rare.

Ely, as a civic servant, didn't need to make an appointment to visit Arthur, but he had his own reasons for not visiting as often as he knew he should.

"I thought that having family to visit was the reason why people opted to stay here rather than going to Tower-Thirteen, but I don't think I've ever seen anyone visit," Ely said as the two men walked into the room.

"Really? I think that just shows you don't visit often enough. We had a girl in here, oh, let me see now... yes, about three weeks ago. A visitor for Violet Truro. Her granddaughter, I think it was. Nice girl. Very polite. Didn't like the view, though."

Arthur gestured towards the exterior wall. Unlike everywhere else in Tower-One, the windows weren't covered in the piezoelectric panels that captured the energy of the wind and rain. Ely watched the incessant raindrops impact against the glass in an explosion that seemed almost to have a pattern to it.

"But then," Arthur went on, "how many people really are close to their families? I mean, take you for example. Your parents were up here, weren't they?"

"I suppose so."

"Did you ever visit them?"

"Well, no. I was moved into the apartments when I was twelve. I don't think I saw them after that. Except in passing, of course."

"Exactly. We're all family now," Arthur said. "Those old bonds, they don't mean as much as they did. I think that will change for those of us who get to Mars, but for now it's just one more luxury we can't afford. I know Cornwall wants to change things. Getting everyone to change their names, that's part of it. But it's going to take more than that to create bonds of affection. It's sad, but necessary."

"Hmm," Ely murmured noncommittally. "But you have to admit, though, that the view is off-putting."

"Don't tell me you're going to start with the whole 'it's unnatural' business again. That's the problem with young people today. You don't think about the past. To you it's just words in books and pictures on screens. You don't remember what it was like."

"Of course not. We weren't there."

"I was speaking figuratively. You don't need to remind me that I'm the last person in this Tower old enough to remember the Great Disaster."

"There's a few others here who were bred before, though," Ely said, looking around at the retirees tending the allotments.

"Born, Ely, not bred," Arthur corrected him. "But they were just children. All they've ever known is the Tower. For them, life hasn't changed much these last six decades. They're just the same as you. They speak of the Great Disaster as if it was one single cataclysmic event. It wasn't like that. We weren't living in luxury one day, with the world collapsing the next. Invasion, occupation, civil war, drought, and famines and plagues. Each year it got worse, but it happened so slowly that no one noticed how bad it was getting until it was too late. And now there's nothing but rain."

They stood for a moment in silence, staring at the large windows.

"Does it ever stop?" Ely asked.

"No, not really, but some days, some times, you can see an errant beam of sunlight reaching down through the clouds. Believe me, this is better than it was before. Then we just looked out on a desert of blistering heat. No vegetation, no buildings, nothing but dust and dunes. Now that was truly depressing. Not that it wouldn't be nice to see the sun properly once in a while, but the world is the way it is. Now, come on, let's go and sit down, and you can tell me about these murders. I hear you've arrested someone."

"I had to let him go."

"Oh?" Arthur ushered Ely into his small unit. "Wasn't he guilty?"

"He was guilty of something, just not anything to do with the murder."

"So why did you interrogate him? I mean, I saw it on the news. I think everyone must know about it by now."

"It's the Chancellor. She... I don't know. She threatened to reassign me. She's making out the murders are my fault."

"You see, lad, this is why I said you should have come to me. You told me you wanted a career in politics one day, and for that you've got to know how to use people. Now, sit down."

Arthur pointed to the only chair. The unit was six feet and six inches wide, ten feet deep, and eight feet high, not much bigger than the room Ely himself occupied. It was identical to the other units on the level except in two respects. The first was that, being at the end, it was six inches wider than the rest. The other was that there was no sleep-pod. Instead there was a simple cot with a plastic frame. On top of it was a single, threadbare blanket. Next to the cot was a small table. On top was a heating element on which something in a saucepan bubbled away.

"I had to give up the sleep-pod so I'd have the electricity to run my little stove," Arthur said. "Well, the council asked for a volunteer. Said they needed to know if any of the food we grow is actually edible. Of course, no one else up here wanted to take the risk of eating it. Not that any of 'em would know what proper food is meant to taste like. So I did what they asked, I volunteered. It was my duty, wasn't it? And they gave me the stove and took away the pod. They say there's not enough energy to run both. Not that I mind. Not really. I don't sleep much these days, but they could have told me up front that was going to be the deal. That's government for you. Never changes. Did you know that these Towers were built to house politicians?"

"Were they?" Ely hadn't known that.

"Back during the collapse. Or before the collapse, in that time when they knew it was coming, but after they'd given up trying to do anything about it. They picked this spot for the Towers because it was out of the way. It was the most remote place they controlled. It was those same politicians who started building the colony ships. If you ask me, I think they'd given up on the Earth and all of us inhabitants by then. They'd decided it was too much effort trying to make things right, and thought they could start again somewhere new. They tried to keep it secret, but you can't keep those kinds of secrets, not forever. People found out, and that's when the end began. I mean, why should anyone work when the effort is going to save others but not themselves?"

"You do it for the City," Ely said, "for the good of the people."

"That's just words, and they're easy to say. It's different when you're actually faced with the choice. After the Great Disaster, it was years before it was safe enough for any of us to venture outside, and it took more years to repair the launch site and salvage what was left of the ships. Sixty long, hard years just to get three ships nearly finished. And in that time we've become cut off from one another. Each Tower's become a City in its own right. They've each become a community, and we've become stronger because of it. Well, adversity can do that, I suppose."

"I know this," Ely said. "Or some of it. But what has it got to do with the murders?"

"Just listen. When it came to it, the government, all those politicians, they didn't make it here. Or if they did, they stayed outside. After what they'd done, we weren't going to let them in. We sealed off the Towers, just like they were planning to. And we did it just in time, just before that final attack. Everyone outside died. Everyone up here survived. Less than one percent of one percent of our species."

"And the ghosts."

"What?"

"You know, the people who got into the tunnels between the Towers. Maybe that's what happened to all those politicians."

"Lad, those are just stories. Legends. They're not real. If they were, do you not think we'd have seen them?"

"No, I know, Sorry, I was just trying to... it doesn't matter. But what's the history of the Towers got to do with the murders."

"Directly? Nothing. Indirectly, well, we'll see. Now, these murders, tell me what you know."

"Well, the victims were the Greenes. They were a married couple who worked—"

"Yes, yes. The parents were killed, the children weren't. You pulled a suspect out of the Assembly just before shift-change. Tell me something I can't get from the news. What made you suspect that man you interrogated?"

"The night-side door to Unit 6-4-17 opened at three a.m. It closed again just over three and a half minutes later. At around the same time the suspect, Glastonbury, went off-net. It's too big a coincidence for that to have happened at the same time as the Greenes were murdered."

"And what evidence do you have that the murders took place at three o'clock?" Arthur asked.

"I told you. That was when the door opened."

"Right, right. And what did I teach you? What does the door opening actually prove?"

Ely hesitated. "Ok, that just proves that's when the door opened, and alright, I can't be sure that was when the murders took place. But again, if it wasn't, that would be a big coincidence."

"And yet, you tell me this other coincidence, this one with Glastonbury being off-net, that that had nothing to do with the murder?"

"Ah, yes. I see what you mean. You're saying two coincidences in one night can't be any coincidence at all."

"Well, maybe," Arthur said. "We'll come back to that. What happened to the bodies?"

"They were sent to Tower-Thirteen for autopsy."

"Fine. Good. Well, that should confirm the time of death for you. Of course, that will take time, won't it? Now as I understand it, no alarms were sounded when the couple died."

"That's right," Ely replied.

"Well, since they clearly did die, that means that someone was able to tamper with the pods."

"Yes, I've got Vox looking into it."

"Vox?"

"Vauxhall, the Controller."

"Ah, right. And do you trust her?" Arthur asked.

"I don't see any reason why I shouldn't."

"Come on, Ely. You just agreed someone was able to tamper with the system. She's the most likely suspect isn't she?"

"Not really. I know that she has the ability to do it, but she's also got the ability to cover her own tracks. She wouldn't have arranged it so the only evidence pointed directly at herself."

"Are you sure?"

"Yes," Ely said, firmly, "I am. She's checking the logs, working out how and when the system was hacked. Maybe that'll show us whether the door-logs were changed."

"Well, I expect she won't be able to find that out quickly. But it's important you know whom you can trust. What else do you know?"

"There were no fingerprints." Ely didn't want to admit he had forgotten to look for them. "But two weeks ago, someone went into that unit and moved the camera. They turned it to face the wall, and they did it whilst the occupants were asleep. That had to have been done by the killer."

"Does it?" Arthur asked.

"What were you saying about coincidences?"

"After nearly sixty years with nothing more serious than a few fights, there are two sets of crimes discovered on the same night. Of course they're connected. I'm asking whether it was done by the same person. Was the killer acting alone? What else have you found out? What about the weapon?"

"Their deaths must have happened so quickly that it had to have been a large heavy blade, something with a handle at each end, pressed down on the neck with a sort of chopping motion. And where are you going to hide that in clothes like these?" He plucked at his jumpsuit. "I can't see how the killer could have gone wandering the halls with something like that, so I think it was disposed of in the chute."

"Hmm," Arthur said with a sigh. "Then look at it the other way. If they carried it into the room, then they could have got it out of there, right? So if you want to know where it's hidden now, start thinking about where it was hidden before the crime."

"You don't think it was destroyed?"

"I can't think of any reason why it would be. So there, that's a part of the puzzle that you can solve. Find where the weapon could be hidden, find out who went there. But that'll take time as well. Is there anything else? Any other evidence."

"Well, it's more the absence of evidence. No one appears on the cameras. Vox has gone through the schematics and thinks it's possible, if it's timed correctly, for someone to walk down the corridor without being recorded."

"And how much time did she spend doing that?"

"What? I don't know."

"See, it occurs to me, that you're being led to think in a particular way here. You've got to distinguish between evidence and conjecture. You say that this suspect, Glastonbury, he had nothing to do with the murder?"

"He was just stealing hot water."

"He was doing what?" Arthur exclaimed.

"Sorry," Ely said, realising how dismissive he'd sounded of the crime, "He'd found that the system recording hot water usage resets itself between three a.m. and half past every day. That's why he woke up. He was off-net because he was in the shower."

"Ah. Wasting energy like that is a serious crime regardless of anything else that's going on. I mean, here I am, giving up a good night's sleep so I can stew up leaves and roots on that stove, and here's someone stealing energy just for his own pleasure."

"Not just him, there are forty-six others doing the same. It's been going on for a year, and there's not a single mention of it on the other-net. They managed to spread the word amongst themselves without me ever knowing."

"That is very serious. So, who told Glastonbury about this?"

"I... I didn't ask."

"Oh, come on lad, that's not how I taught you."

"But does it have anything to do with the murders?"

"Think for a moment. Just sit and think, and then you tell me."

Ely thought.

"Alright," he said. "No matter what time the murders took place, there was no way of covering up the fact that they had happened."

"No."

"I mean, even if you got rid of the bodies, there would be two missing people, right?"

"So?"

"So if they did happen at three a.m., then why pick that time? And if it wasn't at three a.m., but the killer had a way of altering the logs, then why pick that time to have me investigate?" And then Ely understood where the older man had been leading him. "Either the killer knew about the theft of this water and chose that time on purpose, or at least one of those forty-seven is involved and chose that time to ensure there were so many suspects I couldn't possibly interview them all."

"And that, my lad, sounds more right than you know," Arthur said.

"But why?" Ely asked, not really listening to the old man's comment. "I mean why bother going to all that trouble? The autopsy results will come back, and no matter whether they alter or delete some of the camera footage, they can't get rid of all of it. It's just a matter of time before I work out the truth."

"Exactly. That's what I'm saying. That's the answer to all these riddles."

Ely looked at him blankly.

"Time," Arthur said. "That's what this is all about. Or timing."

"Timing? Timing of what? Wait, are you saying this has something to do with the election?"

"Oh no," Arthur said, glancing over at Ely's helmet. "I'm not suggesting anything of the kind. Come on, why don't we go for a stroll? There was a kink in the irrigation system yesterday. Almost flooded the radishes. Leave your helmet though. You keep shifting it around."

Leaving his helmet, with its camera and microphones, by Arthur's cot, Ely followed the old man out of the small chamber, towards the allotments.

"So who do you think—" Ely began.

"In there," Arthur said loudly, pointing to an allotment where two other retirees were dismantling the opaque panelling surrounding it, "are the radishes. Of course, we can't stimulate the gravity on Mars, but otherwise we've got the conditions just like they'll be ten years after the completion of the first stage of terraforming. Not that nutritious, radishes, but if we can get the principles right for them, then we can apply it to potatoes and carrots. That's the theory. Not my theory, I hasten to add, and not one I agree with."

"Arthur, this killer—" Ely tried again.

"Not here, come on." Arthur led Ely past another group working on a different allotment. "Peppery things, radishes. Of course, you won't ever've tried one. You must come up when they're ready. If they're ever ready. The trouble is, that without insects to churn and digest it, we've been having difficulty getting the soil right. Hence the new irrigation system, which breaks down half the time. I said we should try and grow some worms. I was turned down. They said that it would work or it wouldn't, whether here or on Mars. I said it would work better if we'd practiced it first. They just refused. So I doubt we'll ever get any radishes. Shame that." Arthur looked around. They were passed the sealed-in allotments, near the windows. There were no other retirees close by.

"Now," he said, quietly, "it seems like you've got two sets of crimes here. Two very serious ones. Take all these little pieces you've got and put them together. You agree that, sooner or later, it's only a matter of time before you know exactly when the crime happened?"

"At most, it will take a few days," Ely replied.

"So you won't find out until after the election. Tell me, why are you up here with me, now? I mean, why aren't you going busy interrogating each of your forty-seven suspects?"

"Chancellor Stirling wouldn't allow it. She said I could only interview five of them. I've blown one of those interviews already. I wanted some, well..." He was going to say 'help' but changed his mind. "...something more concrete, before I wasted any more."

"Well, alright, what do you think is the most important thing that's happened because of these crimes?"

"The impact on production," Ely answered automatically, "We've lost two workers. And then there's all that energy wasted on heating water It's not just sabotage, it's got to be some kind of wide-spread anti-production sentiment or..."

"No, no, no. I taught you better than that. Sabotage is just another way of describing the outcome. Forget the bodies and the blood and the loss of production. Think about motive. Who benefits from you not being able to interrogate whoever you want?"

"Well, the killer."

"No, Ely, that's just another label. Think! They've stopped all the transport to and from the Tower, haven't they? I've still got my contacts, people still tell me things. No transports in or out until the killer is caught, right? That's the most significant thing that's happened. As to which is the most serious crime, it's not the murders. It's not that those people stole the hot water. It's that for the last year, they've been communicating without being monitored. How they're doing it is something you could solve just by interrogating them. Which you can't do. So, tell me. Who benefits from that?"

"You're suggesting... I mean, I think you're saying that this has something to do with Chancellor Stirling, I just don't see why."

Arthur sighed.

"As soon as the council learns that people are communicating, no, conspiring, off-net, they'll cut Tower-One off completely from the rest of the city. It'll be quarantined, and Cornwall's name will be removed from the ballot. Which means, at this stage, Stirling will win by default."

"You're saying that she wants to hold on to power so badly, that she'd... what? Set up a murder so that I'd discover this theft of the hot water, and that she'd have a reason to close off the Tower?"

"I think," Arthur said slowly, "that she's probably the one who found out about this glitch with the showers in the first place. She's got agents in this Tower, she'll have arranged for those forty-seven people to have discovered the flaw in the system. The murders are simply a way to ensure the offence was brought to light, just at the right time."

"No," Ely said, "it's too farfetched. Why would she do that?"

"Because she's old," Arthur said, softly. "Now listen, and listen carefully. I hear rumours. Good solid rumours that can be trusted. The nurses speak to the pilots when they come to ferry people to Tower-Thirteen. Those same pilots spend most of their lives travelling between our City and the launch pad. Did you ever wonder why people don't come back?"

"Vox told me. They had their sentences commuted if they volunteered to stay on and work there."

"That's what she told you? Well, perhaps that's what she was told and perhaps that's what she believed. It's not true."

"It's not? What happens to them? Do they die?"

"No. It's nothing like that. One of the pilots brought me back a message. There was this man, convicted years ago. It doesn't matter what for. He had a son, still here in the Tower. Each time the pilot came in, this felon would beg for this letter to be brought back and given to his son. Eventually the pilot agreed but instead of delivering it, he brought it to me."

"And what does the letter say? Can I see it?"

"I mulched it. It was too dangerous to be left lying around, even here. But I can tell you what it said. There are three ships being constructed at the launch site."

"I know that—" Ely began.

"Listen," Arthur interrupted, "Three ships. One for each City. The City of Britain will only get one. And that one ship will only make one trip. One thousand people from each City will leave Earth, Ely. Three thousand people in total, and that's all."

Ely had a thousand questions but all he could manage asking was, "Why?"

"That was the plan all along," Arthur said. "There weren't the resources to build ships that could travel back and forth between the planets like they told us. Not enough fuel, not enough parts, not enough raw materials and not enough time to turn them into ships. Three thousand people, that's all. And only one thousand from our City. Half of those places have already been allocated to the engineers and scientists and politicians. There's going to be a lottery for four hundred seats reserved for the guards, convicts and volunteers working at the site. That lottery was the only way of keeping everyone working. That man, the convict who sent the letter, he actually instructed his son to commit some crime so he'd be sent to work on the launch site, because there are better odds of winning the lottery there than here. And that only leaves one hundred places for all the workers in all of the Towers in the City."

"That's..."

"That is our harsh reality. Politicians get a seat. Old people don't. I won't be going. If Stirling loses that election, then nor will she. Nor will you. As a Constable, you're not going to be eligible for the lottery. As a civic servant, it's down to the Chancellor to decide if you get a place, but I want you on that ship, and I think there might be a way. But to do it, you're going to need to solve this murder."

"Just one ship..." Ely murmured.

"Right. Just one. And just one chance for you to live. You remember what I said about when these Towers were built? The truth can't be hidden forever. People will find out, they'll riot. They will tear this place apart and it won't matter. You can't alter the facts. They'll seal off the Towers. Seal off the whole City if needs be, and fill that ship with convicts. Then you won't stand a chance. So like I said, you need to catch a killer. You need to do it publicly. Make everyone see that you're protecting them, that you're keeping them safe. You remember how Cornwall got elected? How he wasn't on the ballot, but people just wrote his name on it. They did it because he was popular. In a place where nothing ever happens, he was famous. You remember? That's how he got elected, and you've got to do the same. You'll be elected by popular acclaim. You'll beat Henley to become Cornwall's successor as Councillor of Tower-One. And then you'll have a seat on the ship. And if you don't get enough votes, then maybe, since you'll have secured Cornwall's place as Chancellor, he'll give you a seat because he thinks he needs you."

"You want me to get elected?"

"Oh, it's not hard. Cornwall proved that. You just need to be popular. You just need everyone to know your name. And they will, if they think you've caught the killer."

"But how am I going to do that. I mean, if you're right, then regardless of who actually committed the murders, the person behind it all was the Chancellor. I can't go and arrest her."

"Of course not, you've got no proof. To permanently seal off Tower-One and stop Cornwall from standing in the election, Stirling will need the approval of the entire council. They won't give it to her if the criminal has been caught and brought to justice. Any criminal. You've got forty-seven suspects. One of them is Stirling's agent. Possibly there's more than one person involved. So pick one, or two, or however many you like. Charge them, and carry out the sentence."

"But what about justice, you always said..."

"There's a bigger justice at stake, here Ely. It's about who leads the human race from this day forwards. Do you want it to be a coldblooded murderer like Stirling? No, Ely, this isn't just your only chance, it's the only chance for our species."

"But what if I pick the wrong person."

"You said it yourself, they're all guilty. And they're all going to die. It's inevitable. Please Ely, if you won't do it for me, then do it for the good of humanity. Do it for the future."

A few minutes later, after he'd bid goodbye to the older man, Ely stood outside the entrance to the Twilight Room, thinking. He understood what Arthur had been saying, but it wasn't as easy as simply picking a suspect. What about truth? What about justice? They were important, even now. They had to be. They were what he'd based his life around.

Up until a few minutes ago, his future had been certain. He had known that one day he would get to Mars. He knew there was something ahead, something that made the daily sacrifices worthwhile. He felt a sudden waive of bitterness that it had been taken away from him.

If Arthur was correct, and Ely saw no reason to believe he wasn't, then Stirling was the one behind it all. He couldn't touch her. He couldn't even order a transport to take him over to Tower-Thirteen so he could arrest her. But if he didn't stop her, and if she somehow won the election, then the future of humanity would be in the hands of a scheming murderer. No, he couldn't allow that. Arthur was right, or half right. Ely could do something, he could bring justice to the people who had aided her. They would be the ones he would execute.

The question that remained, and the one he'd hoped Arthur might be able to answer, was how did he work out who was guilty? He couldn't imagine all forty-seven had been involved. He considered interviewing Glastonbury again. The man had broken easily enough, and Ely was sure he could get a name from him, but that name would just lead to another and another. There wasn't time to go through all the suspects. Then the obvious course of action came to him.

"Control?"

"Yes, Ely."

"Can you go back over the water usage for these forty-seven suspects, go back right to the beginning and find out which one of them knew first?"

"Of course. That's simple enough, but it's going to take some time."

"How long?"

"An hour. Maybe Two."

"Fine." He would still be able to interview someone before shift-change and they went to sleep. He could wake them, of course, but if Arthur was right, then Ely needed to make each arrest as public as possible.

He reached the elevator, but hesitated before stepping inside. To the left lay the museum. Few people ever went in there. Ely certainly didn't. Something Arthur had said came back to him. Where had the weapon been hidden before it was used? If Stirling was involved then, originally, it had probably come from Tower-Thirteen. Even so, it would still have had to have been stored somewhere. The museum would be an ideal hiding place. And then Ely remembered something else Arthur had said, that there was no reason for the weapon to have been destroyed. But the only reason not to dispose of it would be if more murders were planned. He had to find that weapon. Ely went into the museum.

Fifteen years ago, before the increased energy demand had necessitated the expansion of the Recreation Room, each artefact and exhibit, had had its own space. Now they were all crammed together haphazardly in a room barely big enough. Statues, relics, paintings, icons, some ancient, others merely old, were stacked indiscriminately with no explanation given as to what they had once been, nor why it was important that they were preserved.

Like the Twilight Room next door, anyone could visit the museum as long as they made an appointment in advance. Ely brought up the records. The last request had been five months ago, made by Simon Greene, son of the murder victims. He checked and found that was the only time the boy had visited the museum. Neither his sister nor his parents had ever visited. He stared at the name for a moment. It had to mean something, though he couldn't think what. He dismissed the record from his display and returned to his search for the weapon's hiding place.

Museum was the wrong word. It was a storeroom, and one that, the more he looked, seemed to be absent of any metal. He recalled something he had read in one of the newsfeeds, something about some ancient crown being melted down to be turned into circuitry for the ships. He'd not read any further than that, his interest in history extended only to those brief few decades where mankind had produced movies.

He picked a path between the objects, knocking against some and scratching others as he ventured further into the gloom. There were no walkways, just a gap between the objects, left there when the room had been filled. As it was so rarely visited, only a quarter of the room's lighting panels were on. Most of those were blocked by the statues and ornaments that had been piled up to the low ceiling. He turned the helmet's emergency light on. It helped, a little.

He peered over and under and behind the carvings and paintings. He picked up and discarded jars and vases, one after another. He clambered over a large stone block, inscribed with incomprehensible markings, and then he stopped. There were thousands of places within the museum in which the weapon could be hidden, but wherever it was, the killer needed to have quick access to it. That meant it had to be close to the door. He turned around and began to head back. But then he noticed the statue.

It depicted a woman, staring upwards, her hands held out in supplication. Hanging from one of her hands was a ribbon. All the other artefacts nearby had been moved, clearing a space around it. Squeezing past a marble plinth, Ely moved closer. It wasn't one of the older statues in the room, but still showed at least a few centuries of wear. The ribbon, on the other hand, was far newer, woven together out of red and blue fibres.

It hadn't been printed, Ely realised, it had been *made*. It was of a crude construction, but weaving it would still have taken someone's precious time. He took another step closer. He reached his hand out towards the ribbon.

There was a sudden loud bang. A painting behind him ripped. Turning, he looked for the source of the noise. Something deep in his memory stirred. He knew what the sound was, or he once had. He thought the noise had come from near the door. He took a step towards it. He could see nothing in the gloom.

There was another bang. Something whistled through the air, inches from his head.

A bullet. A gun. Someone was shooting at him. He dived for cover behind the marble plinth.

There was another shot, accompanied by the sound of splintering stone. Someone was trying to kill him. It was the murderer. It had to be.

Galvanised by fear, he brought up the image recorded by his camera after that first shot. It was too dark to see anything. He tapped out a command, trying to sharpen the image. Yes, there was someone just to the right of the doorway, but there wasn't enough light to see their features. He'd worry about that later. There was only one thing he could do, he had to get to the door, and stop the killer from getting out of the room. He looked around, trying to find a place where he could climb over the exhibits.

There wasn't one that wouldn't leave him exposed. He needed a distraction. He looked back at the statue. He'd topple it over, and hope that gave him the few seconds he needed. He crouched, turned, and dived towards it.

There was another bang. A splintering of ceramic. A heavy weight fell on the back of his head.

Everything went white, then dark.

Chapter 6 - The Infirmary
Twelve hours before the election

"Can you hear me?"

Ely tried to say 'yes', but the words got caught somewhere at the back of his throat.

"Constable? Can you hear me? Can you speak?"

Of course, he tried to say. The words didn't come out.

Everything went quiet.

"Is this Tower-Thirteen?" Ely asked. He knew it was him asking. He recognised the voice.

"No son. You're still with us."

He knew that voice, too. It was the Councillor's. No. Not the Councillor. It was Arthur. And there was something important. Something Arthur had said.

Before Ely could remember what, he passed out again.

"Do you know where you are?"

Ely opened his eyes. He saw Nurse Gower.

"The infirmary. Level Seventy-Seven," he croaked.

"Here, have some water, son," Arthur bent forwards, and held a cup to Ely's lips.

He took a sip. The water tasted like ambrosia.

"Constable, do you know what happened?" the nurse asked.

"I was... I was shot?" Ely replied, uncertainly.

"Hardly," Arthur laughed. "If you had you'd have been shipped off to Tower-Thirteen. Can't do bullet wounds and surgery here. No, you were shot at, certainly, but it was a miss. The bullet hit a statue behind you. It turned out to be hollow. Mostly hollow. It was blown apart. It fell on you. Gave you a concussion."

"How long was I out?"

"Four hours," Arthur said.

Ely nodded.

"Who shot at me?" he asked.

"I was going to ask you that," Arthur replied.

"And you can," Nurse Gower said, "but not until I've assessed whether he's fit to leave here or whether he needs to go to Tower-Thirteen for more tests."

"He's fine," Arthur said jovially. "As fit as ever. He was just taking advantage of the chance to get some sleep. That's how you can tell he's a real Copper."

The nurse opened her mouth to argue, then closed it again. She shrugged and walked off to the small office.

"Now, son, what did you see?" Arthur asked, kindly.

"All I saw was shadows," Ely said. "What about the cameras, didn't they catch someone?"

"And that," Arthur said as he tapped a command into his wristboard, "is a very good question. Can you see this?"

Ely had to twist on the bed to see the screen on the small room's wall.

"Here, let me help you. There. You see it. That's you leaving the Twilight Room, right?"

Ely watched himself walk towards the elevator.

"You pause there for a moment, then you decide to go into the museum. Why'd you do that, by the way? I thought you were going to arrest your suspects."

"I was looking for where they hid the weapon."

"Did you find it?"

"I didn't really get a chance to look."

"Oh. Never mind. So, here, that's you going inside, and then... here." He froze the image. "See that shadow, that's your assailant."

"That's all we've got?"

"Wait, it gets better. You know how there are no cameras in the Twilight Room? Well, up until four years ago that entire floor was given over to the retirees. You know what that means?"

"There are no cameras on Level Seventy-Six?"

"So there's none inside the museum. Just a few around the elevator. All we've got to go on is the camera on your visor." He tapped the screen. "And these are the best images we've got."

Ely peered at the picture. The figure was indistinct.

"I can't even tell if that's a man or a woman," Ely said.

"Me neither. And I wouldn't bother trying to guess. Now, this is where it gets interesting. Here, this is the when you were lying on the floor, unconscious. Watch." The image was of a dim section of floor, ceiling, plinths, statues, and the distant doorway, illuminated as much by the light on his helmet as by the panels in the ceiling.

"You see there? I think that's why you're still alive."

"What do you mean?"

"That's someone's shadow. It has to be the killer's, but they couldn't get close enough to you to get a good shot, not without the camera on your helmet recording what they look like."

"What about the cameras by the elevator?"

"No, there's nothing on those. And before you ask, the elevator wasn't used. It looks like the Controller was right. The killer does know where the cameras are, and knows either how to avoid being recorded by them or how to wipe them afterwards. She's going to check whether the images have been tampered with, but I don't think we'll find anything there, not in time."

"And I don't suppose that anyone's wristboard was monitored being in that corridor."

"No."

"Well, what about the bullet?" Hazy memories of one of the old movies came back to him. "Was there a casing left behind?"

"If there was a casing, I expect that was cleaned up by the drones."

"Then I'm no closer to finding out who the killer is."

"I'd say being shot at shows you've got their attention," Arthur said, with a cheerfulness Ely thought was out of place. "If worst comes to worst, we'll just have to wait until they try again. Oh, don't look like that, I was joking."

Ely nodded, and glanced around the infirmary. His helmet was sitting on a table on the far side of the room. Even from that distance he could see that it had a new dent.

"I'll put in the requisition," he murmured.

"It won't be approved," Arthur said, speaking softly.

"Why not?"

"You've got a message on there. From Cornwall."

"I'm not surprised."

"It's not good news. The Councillor has put in a request for extra personnel."

"Where from?"

"Guards from the launch site." Arthur glanced over at Nurse Gower in her office, "they're going to return on the next shuttle."

"But I was shot at."

"According to the Chancellor, you let the killer escape."

"Not on purpose. I didn't have a chance to do anything else."

"It doesn't matter. She's blaming Cornwall, and that's why he's called for reinforcements."

"Then I should tell Cornwall that—" Ely began.

"Shh!" Arthur looked meaningfully over at the helmet, then around the room. "Look, these other Constables won't make it here until after the election. Do you understand? They're going to arrive too late. You've still got a chance. You can catch *a* killer. You remember what I told you?"

"Yes," Ely said. "I do."

"And have you got a plan?"

Ely stared into space for a moment.

"I think so. It's not a very good one, but it might work. I'll need your help, though."

The plan was simple. Vauxhall had identified the worker who'd been stealing the hot water for the longest. Alexandra Penrith. Ely had asked Vauxhall to check where the suspect had been during the shooting. Vauxhall hadn't been able to tell him. The records for the entire shift had been corrupted. She offered to check the camera footage, but that would take time, and that was something that they didn't have.

There was just over an hour until shift-change. Penrith, Glastonbury, and about half of the other suspects were in Lounge-Two, The Sailor's Rest. There was nothing unusual in this. The last round of pre-election broadcasts were being aired.

Despite what Arthur had said, Ely wanted to find those genuinely involved. To do that, he was going to arrest Penrith.

As they rode down in the elevator, Ely checked the location of the suspects.

"There are twenty in Lounge-One, twenty-one in Lounge-Two. The other six are still in Recreation."

"And you want me in Lounge-One?" Arthur asked. "I won't be much use in a fight."

"You won't have to be. It won't come to that," Ely hoped. "You just need to watch. See who runs. See who doesn't. We've got the cameras, but there's not going to be time to analyse the footage before I act."

"Yes, yes. I got that part. You want to see who runs, because you reckon anyone who does is involved."

"What was it you said," Ely began, but he remembered he was wearing the helmet, and its microphone would be recording. "Sometimes you have to take a chance," he finished.

Arthur nodded, knowingly.

"Control,"

"Yes, Ely."

"Are you ready?"

"Ready and watching," she said.

"And are you able to turn those Recreation machines off?"

"Yes, Ely. I just told you I'm ready. If they don't finish Recreation in the next four minutes, the machines they're on will each report a fault. You'll have to hope they decide to go down to the lounge afterwards."

The elevator clanged to a stop.

"What do you think Arthur?" Ely asked as he stepped out of the elevator.

"I think someone will run. The question is who. Good luck." Arthur turned towards Lounge-One. Ely watched him go, then headed into Lounge-Two. He moved towards the wall, and looked at the crowd. He tapped out a command, dimming the wall light above his head.

Standing in the shadows, he slowly surveyed the room. The broadcasts had yet to begin. Some people were talking in low voices, but most were lost in their displays.

With its new dents and the bandages over his scalp, Ely's helmet was a worse fit than ever. He tried focusing on a citizen in the crowd, but the tracking software didn't register the movement. He raised a hand, tilted the helmet slightly until he found a position in which it would work. He needed a new one, but he would never get it. In a few hours, one way or another, it would all be over.

He was certain that it was the killer who had shot at him, and now he was almost as certain that the killer hadn't acted alone. One of them had followed him to the Twilight Room then lain in wait, ready to shoot the moment that he stepped into the elevator. When he hadn't, the killer had become impatient, followed him into the museum, and then lost the opportunity. Someone else had then deleted all the records for that shift. It had to be someone else. Again, they had acted in haste there. Deleting records for the entire shift spoke of a desperation that told Ely he was on the right track. Except...

Except there was a small voice at the back of his head telling him that it didn't add up. His reasoning made sense, it was logical, but it didn't quite fit.

He looked slowly around the room, replaying the events, trying to see what it was that he had missed.

The political broadcasts began. Most of the room's occupants ignored the large screens and stayed glued to their visors where they could follow the running commentary provided by other workers, themselves sitting in front of the same screen mere feet away.

A message came up on his display, 'focus lost. Resetting in 10, 9, 8...' he brought a hand up to move the helmet back into position.

Ely checked the location of the suspects in the lounge. Fifteen were in the main part of the room, five were in the privacy rooms around the lounge's perimeter. He checked that the doors to those rooms were ready to lock on his command.

"Ely? The last of your suspects is leaving Recreation now. The first two have already gone into Lounge-One."

"Why did it take that last one so long to leave?"

"It didn't. I staggered the times at which the machines would report an error. I thought that would look less, well, suspicious."

"Right. Thanks." He hadn't considered that. "And no one is carrying anything?"

"No, it's the same with everyone in the lounge already. No one is hiding anything."

"Good." Then that meant that no one was carrying a gun.

He scanned the room, gauging the crowd, judging the best time to act. Chancellor Stirling was scheduled to be the last person to speak. He couldn't wait that long. Her speech would finish just a few minutes before shift-change. He scanned through the broadcast schedule. Henley was due to speak in five minutes. Disrupting his address would have to do. Ely checked that he had access to the Tower's communication system. He was going to announce the arrest to the entire Tower, and Vauxhall was going to ensure it was transmitted to the rest of the City. He hoped it would work. He hoped someone ran. He hoped...

And then he saw her.

There was nothing unusual about her appearance. Nothing made her stand out. If Ely hadn't been running a full sweep of the room, he doubted he would have noticed her. But whereas every other person in the room appeared on his display with a small tag showing their name, this woman had none.

He focused on her. Nothing. He brought his hand up to his helmet, checking it was firmly in place. He tapped at his wristboard. Nothing. She had no name, no ID.

"Vox," he murmured softly.

"Constable?"

"Can you see what I'm seeing?"

"Hang on, I'm looking at..." There was a sharp intake of breath "It's... it can't..." the Controller stammered into silence.

"What is it? Who is she? Why can't I view her ID?"

"She's... She's... She's a ghost." The Controller stopped, and seemed to get a hold of herself. "It must be her, Ely. That's the killer. She's a ghost, just like I said."

Ely ignored the last comment. It didn't help him and it didn't matter. He started moving towards the woman. Someone had worked out how to delete themselves from the system, he realised. And then he dismissed that thought, and forgot about Penrith and the other suspects. He knew whom he had to arrest.

There was a sudden storm of protest from the crowd. Most of the workers leapt to their feet, shouting and cursing at something the candidate had said.

Ely lost sight of the ghost.

"Vox? Can you see her?"

"Say that again. I can't hear you."

Ely pushed through the crowd, moving towards the last place he'd seen the woman. He knocked a man back down into his seat, and then he spotted her. She was heading towards the door.

He cursed. He should have stayed where he was. He tapped out a command, ordering the doors to close. Nothing happened.

"Vox, close the doors. Close them now!" he barked.

Heads turned to look at him.

"Vox, did you hear me? Close the doors!"

More heads turned, the broadcast forgotten in favour of this more immediate entertainment.

"I'm trying," she snapped back, "but it's not working."

The ghost reached the door. She turned and looked at Ely. She smiled, then disappeared around the corner.

"MOVE!" Ely bellowed. The crowd parted as he pushed his way through them and out into corridor beyond.

"Vox. She's turned left outside the lounge. Are you tracking her?"

"I'm trying, but I'm having to do it manually. I've never done this before."

"She went left, then where?" Ely barked as he reached the doorway.

"Along the hallway, then right at the end."

Ely ran. He turned right.

"Where next?"

"Straight on and... I don't know. I've lost her."

"Well find her!"

He scanned the corridor looking for something, anything that seemed out of place. There, he saw it, an access hatch still partly opened. As he ran towards it he tapped out a command, it had been opened just seconds before.

"Vox, can you lock the access hatches to this ladder?"

"No," she said, her voice thick with panic, "not to any of them."

Ely peered inside and looked upwards. He could just make out a foot disappearing out through a hatch a few levels above.

"Have you got her on camera?" he barked, as he climbed into the hatch.

"I'm trying, I'm trying. It's not easy."

Access ladders, Ely thought as he climbed. They were rarely used, except by him on the few occasions when he had to move around the Tower during shift-change. There were no cameras inside. He should have realised before that this was how the killer had moved so freely through the Tower. He should have realised. But he hadn't. Neither had Vauxhall. Neither had Arthur. He reached the open hatch and climbed out.

He was in one of the Assemblies. A contamination alarm was ringing at this violation of the clean room conditions. A dozen gloved and masked workers, who had been staring at the door, now turned to look at him.

An alert came up at the bottom of his display, recording the hours lost to production the disruption was causing. He tried to ignore it, the chase was more important, but years of conditioning told him that nothing was as important as this loss of hundreds of hours of labour.

He ran out of the Assembly.

"Where now?" he barked into his microphone.

"Take the next right," Vox's voice came clearly through his helmet.

"And then?"

"She's heading towards... towards the elevators."

"Are they locked down?"

"Yes. And they're all still down on Level Four."

Ely automatically began to slow. The ghost was trapped. Only a handful of other civic servants could operate the elevators at will. Except, he thought, this woman had already proved she could access the system. Could she override the elevators? He put on a burst of speed, rounded the corner and there, at the end of the corridor, he saw the ghost. She was levering open the elevator doors.

"Stop!" he yelled.

She turned, and looked at him with that same smile. Then she turned back to the door, and finished levering it apart.

"Stop!" he yelled again, still running towards her.

She did stop, but only because she now had the door open twelve inches.

"Who are you?" he yelled.

She smiled and waved.

Ely suddenly realised what she was about to do.

"Vox where's that elevator?" He was only ten feet away.

"Level Four. I told you."

It wasn't.

The woman took a step through the door, but only fell a few inches to land on the roof of the elevator as it rose up through the shaft. The doors slid shut, and she was lost from view.

"Vox, open those doors. Now!" he screamed as he reached the elevator doors. He slammed his fist into the metal in frustration.

"Stand back," Vauxhall said.

The doors slid open, but it was too late. The shaft was empty. He stuck his head out and looked up. The elevator was already two levels above.

"Call me another elevator!" he yelled into his microphone, as he backed away and started heading around to the next set of doors.

There was a sudden screeching of metal. Through the still open doors, he saw the elevator suddenly plummet down through the shaft. He saw the ghost, still standing on the roof. She wasn't smiling anymore.

"Vox..." Ely began, but before he could finish the sentence there was a deafening crash as the elevator impacted against the bottom of the shaft.

Chapter 7 - Clean up
Ten hours before the election

"Vox, come in. What just happened?" Ely spoke into his throat microphone.

"The brakes on the elevator failed," she replied.

"I know that," he snapped. Then he took a breath. "I mean could she have survived?" He knew the answer even as he asked the question.

"I doubt it, I mean, the cameras are gone. You'll have to go and check for yourself. The elevator is ruined. There's no way we can replace it, but the Tower seems ok. I'm still running a diagnostic check, but I think when they built it, they knew this type of catastrophic failure might happen."

"Right. I see," he said, not really listening. "Who was she? I mean, was she really a..."

"I've got the Chancellor calling," Vauxhall interrupted, "and Councillor Cornwall. I've got to go." She clicked off.

Catastrophic failure was right, Ely thought, as he looked down the shaft. He'd almost caught her. He'd almost had her. If he'd just been a bit faster he would have done, but he was too slow. And now she was dead. He was too far above the wreckage to make out much detail, but he thought he could see a leg. It was very definitely no longer attached to the rest of her body.

Was she the killer? She had been able to override the elevator controls and his command to close the doors to the lounge. She did have access to some of the system. But who was she? Why didn't her records come up on his display? Was she a ghost?

Of course not. It was just shock making him think like that. With a few minutes notice she, or perhaps her associates, had wiped the location data from an entire shift. Someone, probably Chancellor Stirling, had simply erased all record of this woman's existence. And Stirling would have had the access codes to override the elevators and door locks and all the rest. No, he decided, there was no great mystery to it.

He pulled off his helmet and ran his hand across his scalp, pausing when he reached the bandage. Why had she not had the gun on her? Because there was nowhere to hide it whilst wearing the jumpsuit. Then had she been on her way to collect it? He thought of the museum and its rambling collection of exhibits. She must have left it there after shooting at him. That's where she was going, he thought. Up to collect the gun. Where else could she have been going? The transport pad? Could Stirling have sent a transport to rescue her?

He took a breath. He was guessing, letting his imagination get away from him. Well, it didn't matter. She was dead. Just like Arthur had wanted.

He looked at the shaft. The elevator was probably beyond repair. The commuting times would have to be adjusted. Schedules would have to change, perhaps even the amount of time each worker had for sleep would have to be cut. More sacrifices would have to be made. Production would suffer but, of course, that didn't matter any more.

He put his helmet back on and turned around. He wasn't alone in the corridor. The workers from the Assembly had all followed him out. Their names flashed red on his screen, each tagged with a charge of 'dereliction of the workplace'. At the bottom a counter ticked upwards, recording the minutes of production wasted as they stood there watching him. No, not just watching, they were filming and uploading. He checked the newsfeeds. They were all covering this. Even the election broadcasts had stopped.

Ely knew that what he did and said next would determine whether Cornwall would win the election, and thus determine the fate of those few who made it to Mars.

"Back to work. Production can not stop," he said, authoritatively.

"Was that him? Was that the murderer?" one of the workers asked. None of them made any effort to leave.

Ely hesitated before answering, but only briefly.

"It was," he said. "But it was a woman. Not a man. Following a lead, I tracked her to..." He was about to say Lounge-Two, but corrected himself in time. "... The Sailor's Rest. There was a chase, she died."

There was a general murmur of acceptance from the small crowd. Some started muttering a quiet commentary, others typed quickly on their wristboards. Within moments, a dozen new articles appeared, all with headlines on the variation of 'murderer dies in dramatic chase'.

"What about the elevator?" a worker asked.

That was a good question. Ely thought quickly.

"The elevator was destroyed in order to prevent far greater destruction to the Tower itself. It's all over. Get back to work."

And this time they obeyed, backing away slowly in case there was some final piece of drama that they could record. Ely waited until they were gone then headed to the next elevator along. The door wouldn't open to his command.

"Control? What did she do? I can't get the elevator door open."

"That was me. I've shut them all down whilst I run a diagnostic on all the essential systems. You'll have to use the ladders."

Wearily he walked along to the nearest access hatch.

"Vox, do you have any idea who she was?" he asked, as he began the long climb down.

"She's the killer."

"I mean what's her name? Who was she?"

"I don't know."

"Did you get a good image of her face?"

"Dozens."

"And does she come up in the system?"

"Not yet."

"I need to be sure of this. Check to see if anyone is off-net. And run a check on the other Towers as well. We need to know who she was."

"I just told you that. She was the killer."

"How can you be so sure?"

"Because I just watched you tell everyone. It's all over the newsfeeds. Everyone's seen it. The impact woke up most of the people who were asleep. They logged in and checked. Everyone knows, Ely. You caught the killer."

The elevators ran from Level Four up to the top of the Tower. On Level Three, where Ely stood a few minutes later, was the access door to the elevator's machinery.

The door had been blown open by the force of the impact. The walls around it were buckled. The corridor leading up to it, however, was already clean.

Hemispherical drones, each the size of his fist, were swarming around the debris. Some were breaking up the larger chunks whilst others hoovered up the smaller pieces before dashing back to their crevices to empty their load into a recycling chute.

He tapped out a command, and they stopped moving. Careful not to step on any of them, he made his way to the door. He peered through the gap.

The woman's mangled corpse lay motionless amidst tangled wreckage now coated in blood and brain. Ely relaxed. A tension he'd not realised had been there disappeared as he saw that she was, definitely, dead.

That tension soon came back. She hadn't acted alone. What part in her crimes did the forty-seven suspects play? Ely tried to tell himself it didn't matter. Despite his intentions, he'd followed Arthur's advice. He'd found the killer. She was dead. He'd done it all publicly. Everyone was talking about it. Except it did matter. The investigation wasn't over. It couldn't be, not until he had all the answers.

"Vox, can you reprogramme the drones to collect evidence?"

"What for?"

This time he remembered that the call would be monitored and listened to. He thought before he spoke.

"I need to know if the killer was in league with anyone else. There are still those forty-seven suspects, and perhaps there might be some link between her and one of them."

"Well, what is it you want the drones to actually do?"

"We could start with some of her blood. Run her DNA through the system. She might have wiped her own records, but she wouldn't have erased that of her relatives. That would get us a name."

"Well, alright. Anything else?"

"Um. No, not... wait!" he stared down at the body. It was a long shot, but he thought he saw something that might, just might, prove Chancellor Stirling's involvement. "I want a sample of her clothing."

"What? Why?"

"It's the same type of jumpsuit everyone else is wearing. If she lived outside the system, where did she get it from? It had to come from a printer, so which one?"

"I don't see how that will help, but ok." She clicked off.

A few seconds later, whilst he was still looking at the body, a light blinked on his display. He had an incoming call from Councillor Cornwall.

"Yes, sir?" he asked, taking the call. At his feet two drones began to move over the pile of wreckage towards the corpse.

"Well done, Constable. I saw what happened. Well done."

"Thank you sir."

"You found the killer. Not only found her, but dealt with her."

"Sir, I..."

"And, of course, I was wrong," the Councillor said, warmly. "I thought the killer was a man, and I said as much. I'll admit I made a mistake. It does happen, you know."

That was a joke, Ely thought.

"Yes, sir," he said, forcing a smile for the camera a few metres away through which he assumed the Councillor would be watching.

"You caught the killer, and managed it just in time. Well done. The election is ours, Constable. Ours."

Ely noticed the emphasis on that last word.

"Ours, sir?" he dutifully asked.

"Yours and mine. It was very dramatic. Everyone is watching it. I can see here that even those who are meant to be asleep are glued to their displays. Well, a few hours of production lost are to be expected under the circumstances."

"Sir?" Ely couldn't hide the surprise in his voice.

"Oh, come now, Constable. I may preach 'Production First', but there are other aspects to life that are just as important as work. And this night's work is very definitely a cause for celebration. Have you considered a career in politics?"

"I was thinking, perhaps, one day—"

"Well, consider it now. I need good men at my side. There are... details that have not yet been made public. The times are changing and we need citizens of stern resolve, unafraid to act and to do so decisively. We need people like you, Ely. I'm nominating you to go on the ballot."

"Sir..." And suddenly Ely didn't know how to fake surprise. Fortunately, Cornwall seemed to have no interest in what Ely actually had to say.

"No, no arguments," the Councillor said. "You are just what the City needs, and I need people I can rely on in the days to come. I've already told my people to get the word out. Everyone who votes for me, will vote for you, and that will be nearly everyone in the City. Congratulations."

"But, sir," Ely said, though he didn't mean to, the words just came out, "the investigation isn't over yet."

"It isn't?"

"There are still those forty-seven suspects. Someone had to be helping this woman. I mean, why else was she there in the lounge if she wasn't there to make contact with one of them? We should find all the people involved and bring them to justice. All of them."

"Yes, yes, I see. A crackdown. Yes, that could be just what we need. Continue your investigation. But, Constable, I want you to contact me before you question anyone. Voting begins in just over one shift's time. We're set for a remarkable victory. I can't have... I mean, *we* can't have anything upsetting the electorate."

"No sir, I'll speak to you before I interrogate anyone else."

"Good, good. You've a future ahead of you, Constable. One filled with many struggles. Prove yourself up to the task."

Cornwall clicked off.

Ely replayed that last sentence in his head. It seemed a strange way of concluding the conversation. Perhaps that was what the Councillor was like. Ely had never met him in person and up until the last few shifts, had rarely spoken to him. He looked down at the mangled remains of the ghost. Somehow that seemed a more fitting way of describing the unknown woman than 'killer'.

It felt unreal, almost as if, now that it was over, it had all been too easy. The ghost's face was nearly unrecognisable, yet Ely remembered how she had looked. And then he remembered how she had smiled. She had thought that she would get away.

But why had she gone into the lounge? He'd assumed that she had gone there to meet one of the other suspects. Perhaps she had, but she had access to the Tower's surveillance system so surely she would know he was in there. Why then did she go inside? Because he was in there, he realised. She hadn't been going there to meet anyone else. He hadn't been chasing her. He had been following her.

He began to tap out a command, then stopped. He didn't want it recorded. He began to briskly walk along the corridor to the Control Room.

"Ely! Congratulations," Vauxhall began, "I was listening in to—"

"It doesn't matter," he interrupted, taking off his helmet. He checked that it had turned itself off.

"The screens here, can they be monitored?"

"By whom?"

"By anyone. Can we talk privately?" He looked around.

"I told you, there are no cameras down here."

"Right."

"Ely, what is it?" Vauxhall asked, the good cheer gone from her voice.

"There's something wrong, something doesn't add up. Can you bring up the schematics to the corridor outside Unit 6-4-17?" he asked.

"Ok, but tell me why?" she asked as she tapped out a command.

"Which one is the... ok, that's the room the Greenes were murdered in, right?" Ely asked, pointing at the screen.

"Yes. Please, Ely, tell me what's wrong."

"Look, here." He pointed. "There's an access hatch right next to Unit 6-4-17, so the ghost didn't need to avoid the cameras or wipe the footage when she killed the Greenes."

"So? Why does that matter?"

"Well, it's just... I... I don't know." The more he found out, the more he found the evidence didn't quite fit the crime.

"Why didn't the system alert you when the woman walked into the lounge?" he asked, instead.

"I thought I'd explained," she said. "The cameras record everything, but it's the wristboards that tell us where people are. We track those, then search for the footage for that time and place."

"So, because this ghost looks like everyone else you didn't notice anything was wrong?"

"Well, yes. I mean, here." She pointed. "This is the footage from the lounge right now. On this screen, that's the wristboard log. Now, you look at those two and tell me if there's someone who doesn't belong?"

"But we track more than just their location," Ely said. "What about weight and height and gait? What about the motion sensors in the Assemblies that make sure the workers are completing their tasks with the most efficient series of movements?"

"Yes, yes, we've got all that, and I can bring it up, but it's all associated with the workers ID or, to put it another way, the wristboard."

"But on the display on my helmet—" Ely began.

"No," she cut in, "your helmet is different. You get the names and IDs and access to all the records. And you can have that because it's just one screen and one camera. Imagine the computing power, and the requisite energy we'd need, if every camera in the Tower was going to overlay onto every screen here the data for every citizen. We couldn't do it. You understand?"

"I think so, or I'm starting to."

"You know something, or you suspect something, Ely, I can tell. What is it?"

"I'm not sure," he said. "Could the ghost be someone from one of the other Towers?"

"Well..." she paused to think, "... I don't think so."

"You're not certain?" he asked.

"No. I mean... ok. She'd have had to come in via the transport pad, and I watch each delivery and collection. But... yeah, alright. I'm not watching each person come and go. So, possibly. Why?"

He thought about telling her about Stirling, but he wasn't certain they couldn't be overheard.

"I'm just playing around with an idea. What happens when someone dies? Does their record get deleted then?"

"No, it's just removed from the active database. It's still there in the archive."

"So if someone wanted to create a ghost, they would have to go in and actually destroy the entire digital record?"

"Right, exactly, the *entire* record," she said. "For every meal eaten, every shower taken, every hour of Recreation, every time that the wristboard was used would have to be removed. And I don't mean just deleted. That would just make it seem as if the food had disappeared or the electricity was being mysteriously generated by no one. No, you'd have to go through and edit every interaction that person had with the system. I'm not saying it's impossible," she added. "Just that it would take a very long time. I mean, it's almost more believable that this woman was a ghost, you know, living outside the system."

"What, the descendent of someone hiding down in the tunnels for the past sixty years?" Ely scoffed. "I hardly think so."

"Yeah, but the tunnels are like the museum. No one goes there."

"Because they're flooded," Ely said. "No, there's someone else involved in this. Someone who has access to the system, someone who could go in and alter those records. Someone who has the time to do it."

"What are you saying Ely?"

"That I want to get to the bottom of this. I want answers. They're important."

"The ghost's dead. You're going to be elected. What's more important than that?"

"The truth," he said. "Did those drones collect a sample of the woman's clothing?"

"Just like you asked, yes."

"Can you get it analysed?"
"Well, yes."
"I mean right now."

Chapter 8 - Interrogation
Eight hours before the election

It took twenty minutes to find out who had printed the clothing. It took only thirty seconds to get approval from Councillor Cornwall to interrogate her.

"This way," he said as he pushed Alexandra Penrith along the corridor.

"Why? Where are you taking me?"

Ely didn't reply. She had been waiting for her 'home' when he'd stormed down the corridor and pulled her out of the queue. Heads had turned, cameras had begun to record, and a barrage of questions followed them as he marched her down to Level Three.

She kept protesting, and he kept silent, until they reached the corridor with the wrecked elevator.

"I said, where are..." She froze when she saw the debris.

"Here. Do you recognise her?" He pushed her closer to the wreckage, and the body that still lay within it.

"No," she said softly, when she saw the body.

"Who is she?" Ely asked.

"I don't know," she said.

Ely pushed her against the wall.

"Look down at what she's wearing. Go on. Look. Recognise it?"

She glanced down, then hurriedly looked away.

"You should recognise it. Now tell me how you know her!"

"I don't," she said, keeping her eyes resolutely ahead.

"The pattern is unique," Ely said. "They always are. It only took a few minutes to work out who printed it. You did. Five days ago."

"I don't understand. What are you saying?"

"You know that woman. You helped her."

"I didn't. I never met her before."

"You were in the lounge when I tried to arrest her. She was going there to meet you, wasn't she? Tell me why?"

"She wasn't. I really don't..."

"Then explain how she's wearing your clothing."

"How can I? I don't even remember wearing it. I don't remember wearing anything that looked like that. I just select a random pattern every day. The old clothes go into the recycler."

"Which one."

"The one in whichever 'home' I'm allocated of course."

"Really?" He took a step back. "Is that the best you can come up with?"

"I'm telling you the truth."

"You know, if this was the first time your name came up today I might believe you. I might just think this was a coincidence. But it's not the first time. You were awake when the Greenes were killed. Awake and off-net."

"I wasn't—" she began. Ely cut her off.

"You were. I've got the proof. You were in the shower. For twenty minutes. Every night for the past year you've done the same. Except I don't think you were. Who spends twenty minutes in the shower? No, you used that as a cover. How did you learn about the glitch with the hot water? Who told you?"

She stared at him, and he saw the fear in her eyes.

"I know that you found out about it first. And then you told others," he guessed.

Barely perceptibly, there was a tightening of her jaw and a stiffening of her shoulders. Ely nodded. He'd guessed right.

"Who told you about it?" he asked.

He thought, for a moment, she wasn't going to answer. Then she looked around, and seemed to realise that she was truly alone.

"But," she said, "surely you can't think that has anything to do with the murders."

"Tell me."

She hesitated, then glanced again at the body before answering.

"There was a note."

"Where? I've checked your correspondence. You didn't receive one."

"It wasn't in the system. It wasn't digital. It was hand written." Now there was a glint of defiance in her eyes. "It wasn't left for me. It was left stuck in the door to the shower cubicle. Whoever woke first would have seen it."

"What did it say?"

"It just said that anyone could get that extra shower at three a.m. That was all."

"And you told others."

"Yes. So what?"

"Don't you know how much energy that wastes?"

"Like I said," she retorted, "so what?"

He stared at her.

"Was that the only note you received?" he asked.

"You know what? I'm not saying another word," she replied. "So you better just charge me and send me over to Tower-Thirteen and let them send me off to the launch site, because," she leant forwards, and spoke more softly, "I think I have a better chance over there than I do here."

He took another step back. She knew about the colony ships. There must have been another note. He opened his mouth to get her to confirm it, but then he closed it again. The conversation was being recorded. Cornwall would be watching, and Ely wasn't meant to know.

He tapped out a message and sent it to Councillor Cornwall, asking what sentence he should give. A moment later, he received a terse reply.

'Defer sentencing for now. We will deal with it after the election.'

Ely nodded.

"No," he said to Penrith, "I'm not sending you to Tower-Thirteen."

He watched her face and saw her defiance replaced by dismay. And then he was certain she knew.

"You got your confession," Vauxhall said, when Ely returned to the Control Room, ten minutes later. He'd escorted Penrith back to her 'home' in silence.

"Some of it," he said.

"You got enough, surely. You got her to admit her guilt. That means you've got proof on all forty-seven suspects. The killer is dead, what else is there to worry about."

"There's still no connection between Penrith and that ghost," Ely said.

"There's the clothing. That's connection enough, surely."

"Well, what about the system. Can you work out who hacked into it and how?" he asked.

"Does it matter, Ely? I mean, does it really matter? When the next shift starts, the voting will begin and you'll be elected to the council. It's a certainty. Cornwall will be Chancellor, then there will be the ballot for the first of the colony ships. So does it really matter?"

"What if the person behind all this ends up on Mars?" Ely asked.

"So you're determined to keep digging?"

"Voting hasn't started yet. We need to find the connection between Penrith and the ghost. Then we need to find out who wiped the system."

"What if that was the ghost herself? Isn't that the most logical explanation?"

Ely thought of Stirling.

"I don't know. Is it? You tell me?"

"I think you need to sleep. Get some rest, get some food. Look at it again next shift."

"Not yet," Ely said. "I need to find that gun." There were still seven hours until voting began, that meant seven more hours in which Stirling could try to disrupt the election.

Ely returned to the museum and spent an hour looking for the weapon. He couldn't find it. There were so many nooks and crannies that any small object, be it gun or knife, could be hidden and never found. Maybe, he thought, when he was Councillor he could have the room completely emptied out. Then he wondered whom he could trust. And then he remembered that once the election was over, it really wouldn't matter.

He sat down on a stack of stone slabs. A long time ago someone had gone to the trouble of carving the surface into the shape of men on horses chasing one another. Time had worn away most of the features. He picked at the edge of the stone, and asked himself what he was trying to prove, and to whom he was trying to prove it.

The weapon could have been hidden up in the museum. It could have been hidden in one of the access ladders, he rarely used those and knew the other civic servants used them even less than he did. Or it could be down in the tunnels, or the recycling room, or one of the storage rooms. There were, now he thought about it, hundreds of places to hide something that small. He would never find it.

"Control?"

"Ely? Did you find it?"

"No. I don't think I will." He was exhausted. It had been a full day since he'd slept, and less than a shift until voting began. For now, all he could do was hope that the dead ghost was the killer, and any other agents of Stirling's wouldn't have the stomach for murder. "You were right. I'm tired. I'm going to get some sleep."

"Good," she said.

Ely had a small single-occupancy unit down on Level Two. It contained a sleep-pod, a desk, and a chair. He shared a printer, shower and toilet with the other civic servants.

Having a room to himself was considered a luxury and a privilege. It was palatial compared to the units the workers were allocated. Ely hated it. He hadn't slept properly since he'd become a Constable. The lucid dreams induced by the machine were meant to be more restful than normal sleep, yet he couldn't remember the last time he'd woken refreshed.

He looked at the blank walls for a moment. He thought of the Greenes, and their family photograph with the fake Martian background. Ely had no pictures to display. He had no one with whom he could share his hopes for the future.

He sat down heavily in the chair and filled his display with the newsfeeds. He was being hailed as a hero. The articles were singing his praises with a near fanatical hysteria. Even the few pieces that criticised him for destroying the elevator, and the universal view was that he had done it on purpose, had hundreds of comments arguing that the sacrifice had been necessary. It was just as Arthur had said. The timing had been perfect. His victory was assured.

And he didn't care.

He wondered if he would feel differently when he reached Mars. He'd never really thought about what life would be like there. Somehow, it had always been this distant dream, something that was close, but still unattainable. He yawned. He was tired. Whether he would feel better afterwards or not, he needed to sleep.

He took off his helmet and placed it on the desk. He looked at it for a moment. He did need a new one, but he wouldn't get one now. He looked over at his pod. Just a few hours sleep. They said four hours of L-sleep was all that anyone technically needed. Technically.

He checked the time. He'd go to sleep in a moment. Not yet. There was something someone had said. Something important, something that, he was sure, would cause all the pieces to fit together. It was there, just at the edge of recall.

He fell asleep in his chair. For the first time in his life, he didn't dream.

He was woken two hours later by a noise. It was an automated alarm. Blearily he raised his wristboard to his eyes. There had been two more deaths. He grabbed his helmet and pulled it on. He tapped out a command, accessing the cameras. His worst fears were confirmed. It was murder.

Chapter 9 - Ghosts
Four hours before the election

"Out of the way," Ely yelled. His voice didn't carry above the chattering terror of the workers gathered along the corridor. He tapped out a command, sending a message telling the citizens to disperse. No one paid any attention to it.

As he pushed his way to the front of the crowd, he saw that it was far worse than it had appeared on the cameras.

Ten feet from the edge of the crowd lay the body of Nurse Gower. She lay face down, a red stain spreading from a shallow wound in the small of her back. Ely knew that couldn't have killed her. Judging by the pool of blood that surrounded her, there were other wounds on her front.

Twenty feet further on were the open doors to one of the elevators. Just inside, leaning against the wall, lay the body of Nurse Bradford. His throat had been cut. Blood had poured out, soaking his clothing, to pool on the elevator floor.

"Control, come in Control."

There was no answer.

He'd tried to contact her as he'd made his way up to the crime scene but, struggling with trying to wake after insufficient sleep, he'd not thought anything of it when he received no answer.

"Vox. This is Ely. Are you there?"

This time there was a reply.

"Ely? Yes. Yes, I'm here." Her voice was stilted. She sounded scared.

"Can you pull up the footage from when it happened?"

"It... it's been wiped." She spoke so quietly Ely almost couldn't hear her.

"We should have expected they would have done that," he said.

"What? Oh, yes. I suppose," her voice trailed off.

Ely looked around the crowd checking that, as he focused on each worker, names appeared on his display for each one of them.

There was more than one killer. He'd known that, hadn't he? Had this been part of Stirling's plan all along? But this time the victims weren't just workers on the Assembly. As productive as they'd been, the loss of the Greenes was nothing compared to the deaths of these two civic servants.

Thoughts like that wouldn't help, Ely told himself. He needed to find out who had done this, and then he needed to find them, because he now knew that the killer wouldn't stop until he, or she, or they were all dead.

Most of the crowd wore visors. Most of those were now looking directly at him, the little blinking red lights indicating that they were uploading his every move.

"Did anyone see this happen?" he asked.

No one spoke. There was a little shuffling of feet, but otherwise barely any movement. No one wanted to ruin their recording.

"Vox. Someone in this crowd must have seen something. Go back through the footage and find me something. Vox?"

"Yes, yes. I'm doing it now."

"Find me an image of the killer, and find out which way they went."

He turned his attention to the bodies. Moving carefully, so as not to step in the blood, he approached Nurse Gower. He knelt down and looked at her injuries. An inch of thin metal protruded from the wound in the small of her back.

It wasn't a bullet. Nor was it the broken blade of a knife. It was too narrow, and the end appeared smooth, not sheared off. He wasn't sure how the metal had ended up in her back, but he guessed that had been the first wound she had received. From its position, it looked like it had severed her spinal cord.

Carefully, he rolled the body onto its side. He immediately wished he hadn't. Her head lolled back and forth. With a blow similar to the ones which had killed the Greenes, Nurse Gower's head had been nearly completely severed. He wondered what could propel anyone to that kind of savagery.

Gently, he lowered the nurse's body back to the ground. He stood up, and stepped carefully away from the corpse. There was blood on the corridor floor, some small drops, some large, all leading from Nurse Gower to the body of Nurse Bradford.

The small ones, he thought, were Nurse Gower's blood, dripping from the blade. Could the larger ones belong to the killer? No, both trails ended at the body of the male nurse.

He walked over to the elevator and looked down at the body of Nurse Bradford. There was a similar stub of metal, this one protruding from the man's leg. His hands were covered in shallow slashes, as if they had been raised in defence. He had been killed with a slashing cut to the throat, though his wound was not as deep as the one which had killed Nurse Gower.

There was so much blood. So much more blood than had been in the Greenes' pods. Those two had almost looked like they had died in their sleep. Here, the blood had poured out of Nurse Bradford, drenching his clothing. But it had also sprayed up over the walls of the elevator. It must, Ely thought, have covered the killer too.

He looked down the corridor, then at the bodies, and tried to picture what had happened.

The two nurses had been walking, presumably, to the elevator. The killer had then... what? Shot them? The metal protruding from Gower's back and Bradford's leg could be the end of a dart of some kind. Yes, that fit. The killer had shot the two nurses. Gower's spine had been damaged. She had fallen. Bradford had been hit in the leg, but he'd managed to crawl to the elevator, leaving a trail of blood in his wake.

"Vox? Did you get any calls from either of the two nurses? Vox?"

"What? Yes. I mean, no. I mean..." There was a pause. Ely had never heard her sound so discomposed before. "If you're asking me," Vox continued, "whether they called after they'd been attacked, then no, I didn't receive a call. I think, maybe, and I'm not sure, but maybe the communication system might have been hacked. Maybe they tried to call, but it was blocked."

"Can you confirm that?"

"No, I don't know... I mean... I'll try."

"Ok. Thank you, and Vox," he tried to think of something comforting to say, but he couldn't. "Thank you," he repeated, instead.

The killer shot them both. As Bradford was crawling away, the killer had walked along the corridor, reached down to the wounded Nurse Gower, grabbed the woman by the hair, lifted her head up and then cut her throat. Ely looked at the corridor by the woman's body. There was a spray of blood on the wall, about three feet up. Having murdered Nurse Gower, the killer went after Bradford. The male nurse had made it to the elevator, but no further.

He had managed to open the doors. That meant, Ely thought, that whilst the communication system might have been blocked, and the cameras wiped, the killer had no more control over the elevators than any of the civic servants.

Bradford had raised his hands in a futile defence. The killer had slashed at them until reflex or pain had cause the nurse to drop his guard. Then he had been stabbed, the blade twisted, and torn across his neck.

Ely had never liked Nurse Bradford. He'd never liked either of the nurses and that feeling had been mutual, yet he could think of no act either could have committed that warranted such a punishment.

There was a savagery to this attack, one that hadn't been present in the murder of the Greenes. That first wound, the one caused by the dart, would probably have killed Nurse Gower, and possibly Nurse Bradford, long before help could have arrived from one of the other Towers. There was something very wrong about the two deaths. The violence seemed unnecessary.

"Vox, how are you doing with the footage?" he asked.

"I'm working on it." She still sounded agitated.

"Hurry. I don't think these two will be the last."

"What do you mean?" she asked, fear clear in her voice.

Ely understood why. She, or he, would be the next logical target.

"It's only a hunch, but I can't see any reason for the killer to stop. Where's Penrith?"

"Who?"

"The woman I questioned a few hours ago."

"She's asleep," Vauxhall said.

"Are you sure?" he asked.

"Positive."

"What about the..." he began.

"Your other suspects? The same."

He looked up at the crowd. They were still there, still recording.

"You," he pointed at a woman near the front of the crowd, "how did you know to come here?"

Half the heads turned to record the woman and her response.

"How did you know?" Ely asked again.

"I heard. We all did," she said.

"Heard what? A gun shot?"

"No, the screaming."

That was no use.

"Vox, have you any footage yet?"

"Some. Not much. It looks like the killer knows how to wipe the recordings in the fixed cameras, but not the images recorded by the visors. If we knew how that happened—"

"That's not important, not yet," Ely interrupted. "Where did the killer come from, where did they go?"

"It's a man. I've got footage of him disappearing into an access hatch two corridors along."

"Which way?" Ely asked.

"Right," she said.

Ely started to move.

"Follow the elevators," Vauxhall said, "Now take that hallway to the right. That one."

Ely started to run.

"There's a hatch twenty feet in front of you."

"I see it." It was still open. If the killer could erase the recordings of the murder, then why leave footage that showed where he had escaped to?

He reached the hatch, and peered inside. A man stood at the bottom of the ladder, looking up at him. The killer nodded at Ely, opened the hatch at the bottom, and disappeared out into the corridor beyond.

"Vox!" Ely yelled, as he dived through the hatch and began to climb down the ladder. "He's just gone out onto the level below!"

"I see him. He's out in the corridor. He's gone into another hatch."

Ely scrambled down the ladder.

"Can't you seal these hatches?"

"I'm trying. The locks won't respond. The commands don't work." She sounded on the brink of hysteria.

Ely reached the bottom of the ladder and fell out of the hatch into the corridor.

"Where now?" he barked, as he pulled himself to his feet.

"Straight on, there's a hatch about—"

"I see it." It was hanging open.

He reached it, and had his feet on the rung of the ladder before he looked down. He saw the killer, again waiting for him, two levels below.

"He's waiting for me," Ely hissed, as much to himself as to the Controller.

"What? Why?" Vauxhall asked.

But the killer had already gone through the hatch.

"Where's he going, Vox. Where's he going?" Ely barked as he dropped from rung to rung.

"Into the... No, he's stopped at the door."

"The door to what?"

"The Recreation Room. He's just..." hysteria changed to bewilderment, "... looking up at the camera. He's... he's smiling. Now he's gone inside."

Ely continued down the ladder, out the hatch and along the corridor to the Recreation Room. The doors should have opened automatically. They didn't. He swiped his hand down the panel to the side. Nothing happened.

"Vox! Open the door."

"It is open. The system says it's open!"

"Well, it's not," Ely grunted, as he levered the doors open with his hands.

Inside was chaos.

Ely didn't need to ask which way the killer had run. Ordinarily the machines were placed end to end, with a narrow corridor running between them. They had been toppled over. Whether by the killer, or by the panicked citizenry, Ely didn't know. Some workers had been injured, and some of those were trapped underneath the broken machines. With the nurses dead, there would be no one to tend their wounds.

"Vox. Call Tower-Thirteen, we're going to need medical personnel over here," Ely snapped.

There was no response.

"Vox?"

"I heard you," she said.

There was no time for Ely to help anyone, even if he knew how. He ran to the room's other door, through it and out into the corridor on the far side.

"Vox, where did he go?"

"Down the commuter ramp to the lounges."

"Then where?" Ely barked as he ran. He was starting to feel breathless. He was starting to feel tired.

"He's... he's stopped. He's just stopped."

"Where?"

"On the ramp, halfway down to Level Six."

Ely wondered whether, if he stopped to catch his breath, the killer would wait for him. No, he couldn't stop. He couldn't rest. He couldn't risk the chance that the killer would attack someone else. A small voice at the back of his head said that that didn't matter, that almost everyone in the Tower was going to die anyway. He ignored that voice. It *did* matter. He was the Constable. It was *his* Tower and they were *his* people. He had to keep them safe.

He kept running. He vaguely registered that he had past Unit 6-4-17. There was method in the killer's route then, or a message. Ely didn't have the spare breath to work out which. His daily Recreation kept him fit, but it was a long time since he'd properly slept.

"Oh, no," Vox said quietly.

"What?"

"I think he's coming here. To the Control Room."

"Can't you shut the fire doors?"

"I've tried. Don't you think I've tried? None of them will shut. I don't think... I don't know. The door's closed, but if he tries to come in here, I don't think I can stop him."

And Ely didn't think he could reach the Control Room in time. He reached the top of the ramp that led down to Level Three.

"Where is he now, Vox?"

"I'm not sure. Wait..." And when she spoke again, there was relief in her voice. "He's heading down to Level Two..." Vauxhall kept up the directions, and Ely kept up the chase. "...he's on Level One, heading to the recycling tanks. No, he's not. He's going down to The Foundations."

"Which part?" Ely hissed.

"The server room."

That made no sense. Ely had thought, as he followed the man down to the Tower's lower most level, that since the killer hadn't tried to get into the Control Room, he would be heading for the tunnels. But the access point for them was in the Power Plant. The server room had one way in, one way out, and nothing inside but the computers that kept the Tower's systems running. Surely he couldn't simply want to sabotage them.

Ely reached a short stair, pushed open the door at the bottom, and stumbled to a halt in the dark.

"Vox," he hissed, "turn on the lights."

Forbidding darkness turned to a world of menacing shadows as the overhead panels began to glow. Here, where only the civic servants came, and they only seldomly, there was little illumination.

Ely turned around, and around again, turning in quick circles. The killer could be hidden in any of a hundred shadows.

"Vox?" he asked quietly, "are there any cameras down here?"

"No."

That was what he'd thought. The Foundations were split into four quadrants. Each dealt with one of the vital aspects of the City; the Power Plant, the water purification system, air-filtration, and the servers.

"And there's no other way out?"

"No."

"Can you seal us in here?"

"Yes, but I can't guarantee he won't be able to override the lock."

"Do it anyway. And..." he hesitated for a moment, but it had to be done. "Send a message to Cornwall. Tell him we'll need assistance over here. Nurses and Constables. We may need engineers too."

"What? Cornwall. Right."

Ely clicked off, frustrated. The Controller seemed more distracted than ever.

The Foundations got their name from the columns, each two-metres thick and spaced three metres apart, that supported the rest of the Tower. Placed equidistantly between each pillar, turning the cavernous space into a forbiddingly uniform labyrinth, were the servers. From some, red, orange and green blinking lights added ominous colour to the shadows, whilst most sat dark, unlit and unpowered. Great coils of cable snaked out from the servers, along the floor, up the pillars, to disappear into the ceiling.

In the distance he could make out the wall that partitioned this quadrant from the next. In the other direction he could make out the far thicker, and more imposing, wall of the Tower itself.

The air was warm and humming with electricity. Ely shook his head, consigning that noise to the background as he tried to pick out the sounds that shouldn't be there. He couldn't hear any. He turned around. The hum seemed to grow, and as it did, his heart began to beat faster and louder.

"Come out," he yelled. "Surrender. You can't..." he trailed off, unable to think of an adequate way to end that threat.

He couldn't retreat. He had followed the killer down here. The man had wanted him to follow, and from here there was no escape. He must be close, Ely thought.

Ely had been in a few brawls. He could handle himself in a fight. He'd proved that. But he'd had the weight of authority behind his blows. He'd never needed to do more than remind a felon of the fate that awaited those who resisted arrest. He pulled out his truncheon. It seemed a wholly inadequate weapon when compared to the knives the killer had. But he was the Tower's Constable. The two nurses had been murdered. He had to bring them justice.

He thought he heard a noise. It was close. He moved forwards quickly, bringing his truncheon up, holding it diagonally across his chest. He darted past the edge of the pillar and, pivoting and turning, brought the truncheon down with all the force he could bear.

It hit a mess of wires with a dull thud. There was no one there.

He spun around, expecting to see the killer behind him, but no, he was still alone.

Walking on the balls of his feet, ready to dive sideways or forwards or back, he moved slowly past the bank of computers to the edge of the next pillar. Then he darted forwards, turned a full three hundred and sixty degrees, and stopped when he found he was still alone.

He took a breath, then dashed forwards, checking behind the next pillar, and the next, and the next. Again and again, from pillar to pillar, sometimes turning to the left, sometimes to the right, picking a direction when some half imagined sound, magnified by fear, became that of the ghost.

And then he heard it, a scraping of metal. It was so loud it seemed to fill the cavernous space.

He began to stalk towards the noise. It came from the wall. Not from one of the partitions that separated this quadrant from the next, but the twenty-foot thick barrier that protected the Tower from the flooded wasteland beyond.

He began to move faster, his eyes open, ready to dive out of the way of the blow he expected at any second. He reached the wall. The blow didn't come.

A section of metal panel had been removed. It revealed a ladder leading down into the dark.

He stared down into the hole. There wasn't meant to be an entrance to the tunnels here. Yet clearly there was one.

He bent down to look at the panel. The bolts that should have secured it to the wall were smooth. On the tunnel side, someone had affixed a small handle. It could be removed and replaced at any time, but unless you knew where it was, someone could wander down here for days and not find it. It was the perfect hiding place.

And Ely had no reason to follow the killer down there. He could call for tools, and seal the man in. Tower-One would be safe. The other Towers could be alerted, and told to check their own access points. The entire City could be secured.

But that wouldn't be enough. Not for the workers, nor for Ely. Justice, seen or not, had to be done.

He climbed down, into the dark

Chapter 10 - Underground
Three hours before the election

He descended down the dark tube, glancing up at the ever-shrinking circle of light above him. The ladder was pitted with rust. Some rungs were bent. The further he descended, the more he found them covered in slime. He counted forty rungs before his foot touched something solid, rough and uneven. He'd reached the bottom of the ladder. All was darkness. He took out his truncheon.

"Control? Control? Vox, can you hear me?"

There was no answer.

He switched on the visor's emergency light. The beam was weak, stretching out a mere dozen yards. Slowly, he stepped away from the ladder.

There was a crunch behind him.

Before he could turn, something hit him from behind. He fell, hard, dropping the truncheon as he reached his hands out to break the fall. His face hit the ground. His helmet took the brunt of the impact, but he was still dazed.

He rolled onto his side, then onto his back, turning his head this way and that. The helmet's feeble beams of light stabbed out into the darkness as he sought his assailant. He could see no one.

He crabbed backwards a few paces, then staggered to his feet.

"Why did you kill them?" he called out.

"You come down here and that's the first question you ask?" the killer called out. Ely spun around. There was sarcasm in the man's voice, but Ely thought he could tell the direction it had come from. Slowly, tensed, expecting another blow, he moved forwards.

"Who are you?" he asked, after he'd taken two paces.

"That's a good question, but I think you can do better."

The killer was taunting him, Ely thought, but it didn't matter. There was a patch of deeper shadow against a wall three yards away. That, Ely thought, was where the killer stood.

"Surrender," Ely said.

"Oh, no. I don't think so. Not yet." The voice came from behind.

Ely managed to half turn before another blow knocked him sideways. As he fell he saw the killer. In his hands was a long metal pole.

And then the pain began.

His arm had taken the brunt of the swing. He flexed his fingers. No, his arm wasn't broken. He hoped. But he was in more pain than he'd ever felt before.

"Why?" he screamed.

"Why? Why do you think?" the killer asked blithely. He stood ten yards away, at the edge of the beam of light cast by Ely's helmet.

"Do you deny" Ely hissed, "that you killed Nurses Gower and Bradford?"

"Deny? Of course not," he replied. "But isn't there something else you want to ask?"

"No," Ely replied. "I know you've been working for Stirling. You want to undermine Cornwall to win the election. I know about the colony ships, how there's only space for thousand people out of all the citizens in all the Towers. I know all about you."

The man laughed. The tunnel filled with its mocking echoes.

"You haven't a clue, have you? I thought you'd be different. Or are you just the same as the rest? Look about you, and try to understand what you see."

Ely needed a weapon. There was a lump of rubble on the ground two feet away. He edged sideways, hoping he wasn't telegraphing his intentions.

"Ok. I'm listening. You wanted me to follow you down here, so you clearly have something to say. Tell me, then."

"You don't understand," the killer said. But then Ely realised that, no, he hadn't said it. He'd asked it. It had been a question.

"Understand what?" Ely asked, and at the same time, lashed out with his foot, kicking the rubble towards the man. The killer had been expecting it and skipped sideways. Before Ely could move out of the way, the metal pole arced through the air, and hit him in the side of his head.

He fell. His vision blurred. He tried to stand. He couldn't. He knew he had to move. He expected another blow at any moment. It didn't come.

Ely pulled himself up.

One of the helmet's two lights had been shattered. With the light of the remaining one, he searched the gloom for the killer. He couldn't see him.

He listened.

He could hear movement, but it was getting further away.

His light flickered. He slapped the side of his helmet and wished immediately he hadn't. His head swam, but when his vision cleared he saw the beam of light shining down steadily on the floor.

He took a moment to look about, and this time he did it properly. It was a tunnel. He'd expected that. The ladder was situated about halfway along. Behind him, away from the direction the killer had run, was nothing but darkness.

He looked down. He was standing on rough cement, as he'd first thought. What he'd taken to be rubble was actually broken fragments of the tiles that had once covered the floor. Why, during the hectic panic when the Tower was built, had they tiled the floor? That made no sense. Some tiles were ridged, others smooth. There might have been a pattern to them. There was too much debris and mould to be sure.

And the fact there was mould begged another question, but it was forgotten as his light played up the walls. There was a pipe. It ran along the wall, disappearing in each direction. What had it carried? Presumably it was something from, or to, Tower-One, but what? Above it on the ceiling were opaque plastic panels that he guessed were lights, but at regular intervals between them were small metal grills. Was that for air-filtration? That question was, in turn, drowned out by his confusion at the large plastic panels pinned to the wall.

They were like frames, yet they had nothing inside of them. Were they displays? No, he realised as he took a step towards one, they weren't screens. A few ragged edges of the paper that had once, long ago, hung inside, still clung to the edges of the frame.

There was another, a few feet along. He walked towards it. The contents, there too, had decayed. He moved his helmet to play the light up and down the corridor. He spotted some paper inside the frame. He could make out a couple of words; '... your choice, your future.' They had been at the end of the sentence. How that sentence began, he couldn't tell. The only other part of the poster that still survived was an image of a domed roof, topped with a spire.

Why would anyone, during those last desperate years, have put posters up in the tunnels between the Towers? The only logical answer was that it had been done by the ghosts, yet that seemed an unsatisfactory explanation.

There was a noise off in the distance. Ely remembered why he was down there. He put the mystery to one side and began walking down the tunnel in pursuit of the killer.

He walked briskly. Stealth served no purpose when the helmet's light gave away his position. He couldn't turn it off, not simply because the footing was unsound, but because he feared the dark more than the ghost.

The tunnel curved. He saw a small beam of light up ahead. That had to be the killer. Ely picked up his pace, darting his head up and down between the floor and his prey. The light got brighter. He began to jog. The light suddenly spun and fell. The killer had dropped it.

Ely broke into a run.

He made twenty strides before he saw the killer. The man was on his knees, his hands scrabbling for the dropped light.

Ely kept running, turning a stride into a skip, and brought his foot up in a roundhouse kick. His boot smashed into the man's face. The killer flew backwards.

Ely was unbalanced, and toppled more than leapt onto the man, knocking the killer down as he tried to rise.

Ely punched. The killer kicked. Ely bit. The killer pushed and head-butted and managed to get free.

Ely pulled himself back to his feet. The killer was, standing, fists raised, just a few yards away. Blood was pouring from his mouth. Ely thought he might have been about to speak. He didn't give the man the chance. Ely charged.

His shoulder hit the killer squarely in the chest. The man punched and thrashed. Ely screamed and pushed and pushed and kept pushing.

There was a wet crunching sound, and it was the killer's turn to scream. His thrashing stopped, and Ely found that he couldn't push the man any further. He let go and took a step back.

Ely stared. He'd impaled the man on a four-feet long piece of bent metal that jutted out into the room.

"No," he murmured.

The man's eyes met his.

"Who do you work for? Where did you come from?" Ely whispered.

"An eye for an..." The man coughed. "... Beat them... their own game."

"Who sent you?" Ely asked again, his voice rising.

The bubbling cough turned into a rasping laugh. Then it stopped.

"Who..." Ely began, but he didn't finish the question. The man was dead, that smile still on his lips.

Ely took a step backwards, then another, then he collapsed onto the floor. He watched the pool of blood slowly grow around the dead man.

"I'm sorry," he said. "It was an accident. I didn't mean for... I'm sorry."

Minutes passed.

This is a crime scene, Ely thought.

"This is a crime scene," he repeated it out loud, hoping to find some comfort in the sound of a voice amidst the dark. He felt no better.

"I should preserve the scene," he said. "Shouldn't I? But, what for? No one is coming down here. All they want to know is that the killer is dead."

And this man was the killer, and he was certainly dead.

"Why did you do it? What were you trying to tell me?" he asked.

There was no answer, not even from inside Ely's own head.

The adrenaline began to wear off and Ely started to notice his surroundings once more. He got up, painfully. His head ached. His arm ached worse, but he was certain it was just bruised. He looked down, playing the feeble light over his body. His jumpsuit was torn. He had a few scratches, but was otherwise unhurt. He raised his head to look at the corpse once more.

The spike on which the man had been impaled had been part of a support for an open sided metal box. It had been a little larger than the height of a man, and perhaps four feet square. It looked a little, Ely thought, like a sentry post from one of those old movies. A chunk of masonry had fallen from the ceiling, crushing it, causing one of the supports to fracture and twist so it was pointing out into the room.

And was this a room? He looked around. There was something about the space, something almost familiar. He'd never seen the like before, but he thought he'd seen echoes of it somewhere. In a picture, or perhaps a movie? He shook his head, there would be time enough to look around. There was something he had to do first.

He approached the body. Gingerly, he reached out a hand and peeled the cloth away from the wound. The material was wet, warm and sticky with blood. Ely swallowed.

Underneath was not skin, but another layer of material. It was made of something thick and unfamiliar. If it resembled anything he'd ever seen, it was the material covering some of the seats up in the museum.

He peeled away more of the jumpsuit. It was a harness. Strapped to the leather were slots. In each was a small cylinder of metal. He pulled one out. It wasn't a cylinder. It was a metal bolt, about six inches long, with a pointed tip. That, he guessed, was what had been in the nurses' wounds. Under the man's left arm was a sheath. In it was a flat metal handle. He pulled it out. The handle was attached to a blade. The edge was still covered in blood. He dropped the knife.

Holstered under the man's right arm was an L-shaped piece of metal. There was a trigger, but it bore very little resemblance to the pistols he had seen in those old movies. He took it out, and examined it. There were two tubes, one on top of the other. In each, there was already a bolt. He guessed that if he pulled the trigger, a spring inside would propel the bolts out.

It was incontrovertible evidence that this man had killed the two nurses. For want of anywhere else to store it, and after he checked it wasn't liable to go off accidentally, he tucked it into his boot. Would it be sufficient evidence? Would the workers want to see the body as well?

"People need to know they are safe," Ely said. "They need to know they can work and live in... they won't, though, will they? Almost all of them will die. Was that what you were trying to tell me?"

He turned away from the corpse in frustration and looked around to see if his surroundings could give him any answers.

He was in a hall, the walls about fifty feet apart. To his left, the way that he'd come, and to the right, the space disappeared into darkness.

The ceiling was low, just above the reach of his outstretched hand. It had the same pattern of lights and vents that there had been in the corridor, though here there were more gaps. He took a step to one side and shone his light up through one. It wasn't a ceiling, not a proper one. It was made of some thin material above which hung a mess of pipes and wires and brackets.

That was a terrible waste of metal. Everyone knew their stocks were low. The materials down here should have been salvaged. And the space itself, he thought, why was that being wasted?

He walked slowly towards one of the walls, letting the torchlight play up and down the cracked and faded paintwork. There was a wooden door hanging open from its hinges. He took a step forwards. Inside was blocked by rubble. He continued on until he reached another door. This one was closed. He tried the handle. It moved slightly, but the door did not. He stepped back, and shone the light along the wall. There was another corridor, a few yards further on.

"Where am I?" he asked himself, turning around, peering into the gloom beyond the extent of his light. "Corridors and doors. Tunnels and..."

It was a junction, he thought. That had to be it. A place where all the tunnels connecting the thirteen Towers met. That didn't explain the rubble or why there were no signs.

But there were symbols, he realised. And one that appeared more than any other. Once he'd noticed it, he started to see it everywhere, on the doors, the walls, even on the floor; a hollow circle with a thick line running through it. He'd seen it before, in one of those old movies about The War. He couldn't remember which one. On the wall, under the circle, there was some writing. Most of the tiles upon which the lettering had been printed were chipped and broken. But he could still make out the word, 'Underground'.

He kept walking. The place was derelict, but not ruined. The drones could have cleared it up in a matter of hours. People could live down here. The question of space and breeding rights could be solved. Could have been solved, he thought. It was too late now.

The light caught something metallic. Stairs.

He walked towards them. The light reflected off something beyond. It was water, dark and topped with black slime, but water nonetheless.

He felt an enormous sense of relief. The tunnels were flooded, just like he'd been told. For whatever reason the tunnels weren't used, he now felt that there would be a reason.

He was in a junction, then. He'd been turned around in the darkness. All he'd done, he thought, was run around under Tower-One.

He heard a sound, something metallic falling to the ground. He turned his head towards it. The sound came again. The previous moment's relief vanished as he moved towards the noise.

He'd taken four steps when he heard it again. He took another ten steps before the light hit a wall. In it was a door. He wished he'd not left the knife with the body.

"Who's there?" he called out.

There was no answer.

"I'm Constable Ely, from Tower-One. Come out."

He felt foolish as soon as he'd spoken the words. He sought for something else to say.

"I didn't mean to kill him," he said. "It was an accident. But he was a killer. A murderer of innocent people."

The words echoed hollowly in the gloom.

"The City must come first. Production must come first. Our species must come first. All else must wait."

There was silence, until he heard a voice ask, 'Why?' But that voice came from inside his own head.

"His death was an accident," he said again, as he opened the door.

Inside was a short corridor, beyond that a room. He went inside. There was no one else there.

The room was twenty feet wide, twenty feet deep. Against the far wall was another door, this one closed. In the centre of the room was an allotment bed, identical in style though not in construction, to the ones Arthur tended up in the Twilight Room.

The lamps above the plot were all of an irregular manufacture, the tubing of different colours, melted and taped together. The plot was more than half-filled with plants. He didn't recognise any of them. They were ordered in neat rows with those on the left hand side being little more than shoots. As the rows snaked back and forth, the plants grew in height, until they reached a spot on the left hand side where the soil was bare.

There was a metallic clink. A lever spun, a valve was released and water began to fill a reservoir. That was the noise he'd heard, an automated mechanical system for watering the crops. There wasn't anyone else down here.

This was where the ghosts got their food, then. Why? Couldn't Chancellor Stirling have given them food to take with them? Couldn't they have just stolen it? It would have been so much easier than growing it from scratch. He knew that the answer was here, somewhere in this room. This time he would find it.

There was a workbench against one wall. Next to an odd assortment of tools, wires and a stack of metal pipes, all neatly sawn into foot long lengths, was a pile of jumpsuits. He picked one up, then another, then a third. They were of three different sizes.

A light started flashing on his display. A message read 'battery low'.

Three sizes. Three ghosts. And if the third wasn't down here in the tunnels...

He left the room. As he walked back into the hall, his dimming light fell upon the body once more.

He wanted to take it back into the Tower. He wanted to show it to the people. It proved something, though he was unsure what. The warning light began to blink faster. There wasn't time. He would have to come back for it later. He quickly scanned the ground and found the flashlight the ghost had dropped, then he headed back to the tunnel that led to the ladder. The battery on his helmet died just as he reached it.

A few minutes later, after he'd clambered back out of the hatch into The Foundations, his wristboard started to flash with messages. They were all from Vauxhall. His hand hovered over the screen, uncertain what he should tell her. He didn't know whether the third ghost would be able to read the message. He decided to keep it brief. He tapped out, 'The killer is dead. I'm on my way up.'

"What happened to you?" she asked, when Ely entered the Control Room. He was vaguely surprised to see Arthur there.

"There was a fight," he said, taking off his helmet. "The helmet's battery died," he added.

"I got your message, 'the killers are dead'. I've sent it to everyone in the Tower," she said. "It's all over the newsfeeds."

"What? Er, yes, the killer. One killer is dead," Ely corrected her. "But there is another. There were three of them."

"Three? You're sure?" Arthur asked. "And this third one, smaller or larger than the other two?"

"What?" It was a strange question. He thought back to the jumpsuits. "Smaller, I think."

"And a man or a woman?" Arthur asked.

"I'm not sure."

"Think. It's important."

"I've no idea."

Arthur looked over at Vauxhall. They exchanged a look.

"It's what I thought," Arthur said, slowly. "Did that man say anything before he died?"

"Nothing that made any sense," Ely said, he suddenly felt very weary. He sat down heavily in the Control Room's only chair. "Down there," he said, "there's space. There's room. You could fit this entire Control Room. And the Recreation Room, as well."

"Down where?" Vauxhall asked. "You mean down in The Foundations?"

"No. I mean down in the tunnels."

Vauxhall opened her mouth to speak, but Arthur waved her into silence.

"That's where you went?" Arthur asked, "You went down through the hatch in the Power Plant?"

"No, there's a ladder. Down in the far corner of the server room. I think... I don't know. I think they built the Towers on top of the ruins of something else."

"Oh?" Arthur asked, "What kind of ruins did you see?"

"No idea," Ely replied. "It's dank. It's dark. Part of it's flooded, of course, but you could live down there. The ghosts did. And there's metal that could be used. Could have been used," he sighed deeply, "but there's no time now. All these years, Arthur, all those Chancellors, they talked about sacrifice, didn't they? But their efforts were incomplete. They were only ever half-measures. I doubt there's enough there to make another ship, and there's no time now, but maybe one more life could have been saved. And now..." He glanced up at Vauxhall, "I don't think you know, do you? About the colony ships, I mean. You should tell her, Arthur, she deserves to know."

They shared another glance.

"He's... he's already told me," she said.

"Good. Good." Ely suddenly didn't care. He was exhausted. "We need to find this third ghost. Then afterwards... I don't know." He closed his eyes for a moment and tried to think clearly. "I need to speak to Cornwall, maybe we can organise search parties or something."

"Not today," Arthur said. "It's election day, Voting's about to start. And you're set to be elected."

"It doesn't matter," Ely said. "Not anymore."

"No, but finding that ghost does," Arthur said. "No one's safe whilst she's running around. Whatever happens next, Ely, you are still the Tower's Constable. You need to do your duty. You understand?"

"Duty. Yes, I understand. Do you have any idea where I should look? There are—"

He was interrupted by an alarm.

"What's that?" Ely asked.

"That's nothing," Vauxhall said. "It just means the voting has started. Look, I think I've found a way to track the killer," she continued. "They keep hacking into our system, deleting and altering records, right? Well, I think I can monitor the location the changes are made from."

"So we just wait until the ghost decides to—" Ely didn't get to finish the sentence.

There was a muffled bang. The Tower shook.

"What was that?" Arthur asked, running over to the screens. Half had gone blank.

Vauxhall pushed him out of the way.

"There's been an explosion," she said, simply.

"Where?" Ely asked.

"I don't know. Half of the systems have gone offline, including the ones that would tell me."

"Could it be an accident?" Ely asked.

"Of course not," Arthur snapped. "It's her, isn't it?"

"I think it came from down in The Foundations," Vauxhall said.

Ely nodded, thinking that there were a thousand places to hide down there. He'd probably walked right passed the killer without noticing.

There was another explosion, this time far closer. The screens rattled, metal creaked.

"That was recycling tanks," Vauxhall said, as she began pulling up files. "More than half the systems are gone. I've still got access to the sleep-pods, the air-filtration plant, and about half the Tower's lighting system."

"Forget that," Arthur said. "What about the cameras?"

"Some of them... I think..." She tapped out a command.

"There she is." Ely pointed at a screen. A woman, wearing a rough-looking coat, stood staring up at a camera. "Where's that?" he asked.

"That's the airlock on Level Seventy-Seven," Arthur said.

"Then that's where I'm going." Ely stood up.

"Wait," Arthur said. "You'll need this. He took out a package from underneath the desk. It was wrapped in linen, still covered in dirt. "Kept it in the flower beds. Just in case." He unwrapped it.

"A pistol?" Ely took it, cautiously.

"Kept it since the Disaster. Kept it clean. Careful, it's loaded. Never had to use it, not in here, but... Do you know how to use it?"

It was far bulkier than the ones he'd seen in those old movies. It was made of slick black metal, and a plastic far more durable than the Tower's printers could produce.

"This would have been useful a few hours ago," he said.

"I didn't think you needed it then. And you didn't. But there's a time coming and coming soon if I'm any judge, where you'll have to make a choice. This will help you with that choice. There's a catch at the side. You want it pointing straight down when you pull the trigger."

"Right. Got it." Ely grabbed his helmet. The batteries were still flat. He dropped it. "Keep track of me on the cameras. Send me messages to my wristboard, if she moves..."

"Just go, Ely," Vox said. "And good luck."

Ely nodded once, then ran from the room and to the ramp that led up to Level Four.

The Tower was in chaos. The explosions had woken the workers who had been sleeping. Some of them milled about the corridors, others, just like they did every time they woke, were queuing by the elevators. At his approach they began shouting questions. Ely said nothing as he pushed them out of his way.

He reached the elevator, but hesitated before stepping inside. He tapped out a quick message 'do you still control the elevators?'

"Constable? Constable!" One of the workers approached him. Ely ignored the man and sent the message to Vauxhall.

"Constable! I'm talking to you. What's going on?" Ely stared at the man. He could see fear in his eyes. Ely could think of nothing to say. He received a reply from Vauxhall, it simply said, 'Yes'. The door opened. He stepped inside, then put out a hand to stop the man from following him.

"You don't want to come with me," he said.

"But what's happening?"

"Just wait. There will be an announcement soon," Ely said, it didn't seem sufficient. "It's going to be ok."

The doors closed, and Ely hoped he was right.

The doors opened again a few, long, minutes later. Ely saw he wasn't at the top of the Tower, only at the 'farms'. He tapped out a message to Vauxhall, asking her what had happened. There was no response. Fearing the worst, he was tempted to go straight back down the Control Room. He didn't. Something told him to keep going. He ran to the nearest access ladder and began to climb up.

By the time he reached Level Seventy-Seven, the dull ache in his arm had turned to a grinding pain. He ignored it. He was beyond exhaustion. His brain felt numb. All he knew was that he was the Constable. He had to keep the citizens safe.

He reached the top of the final ladder, opened it, and fell out into the corridor leading to the transporter airlock. He got slowly to his feet, and saw the ghost. It was a woman. She was standing thirty feet away from him and ten feet from the airlock. She was waiting.

He fumbled at his waistband and pulled out the pistol.

"Don't move," he said, as he levelled it at her. The barrel wavered slightly.

"Hello Ely," she said calmly. "You took your time."

"Don't move," he said again.

"I'm not," she said.

There was something in her left hand, something small. It appeared to be a handle without a blade. It didn't look like a weapon, but then Ely remembered the L-shaped piece of metal in his boot, and the bolt in Nurse Gower's back. He tightened his grip.

"I suppose you have some questions," she said.

"No, not really."

"Oh, come now," she said. She was smiling, just as the other two ghosts had been, "I can see that you do. You want to know who we are. Who I am. That's what you asked Gabriel."

"Who?"

"The man down in the tunnels. I saw what happened. And you're right, that was an accident. A tragic, stupid accident."

"You were there? You were listening?"

"Of course. We hid in the one place no one would think to look. A place that even they had forgotten about." She took a step towards him.

"I said stop! Don't move," Ely yelled.

"Ok, ok. I've stopped. And what happens next?"

"We'll repair the Tower. We'll undo everything you've done..." Ely began, but then he trailed off.

"You won't," she said. "The Tower's broken. I saw to that. Food can still be grown, and water can be purified, but there won't be the power to run anything else. It's time for the light to be let in. Not that you know what that means."

"It means everyone will die," Ely said.

"Death comes to us all, Ely, but it doesn't have to come to everyone in the Tower today. But what I was asking is what you are going to do next. You can't arrest me."

"There should be a trial."

"Really?" she laughed. "In front of what court? You don't have the authority to arrest me, nor to judge. All you can do is try and kill me, but I promise you this, if you pull that trigger, you will die."

She'd taken another step, Ely realised, but she was still twenty feet away.

"Maybe," he allowed. "But then, so will you."

"No, at this distance, I probably won't." There was a touch of genuine sadness in her voice.

"Lie down," Ely said. He'd had enough. "On the ground. Now."

"You really don't want to ask who I am or what this has all been about?"

He did, but more than that he didn't want to play her game.

"You can answer questions later."

"If you won't listen," she said, as she moved over towards the wall, "then I'll just have to show you. Keep your mouth open."

"I said don't..."

Her hand moved. The doors to the airlock exploded.

All he could see were lights. All he could hear was noise. All he could feel was air rushing past him.

He tried to move. His legs didn't work. No, he realised, they did but he was on his back. There'd been an explosion. Another bomb. He'd been knocked down by the blast.

He rolled onto his side, and felt a jagged piece of metal slice across his cheek. The pain cut through the fog. He pushed himself to his knees. 'Breathe,' he told himself, 'breathe'. And he was breathing. It wasn't hard. He had to get up.

He reached out to brace himself on the wall. He stumbled to his feet. He remembered the ghost. Expecting her to attack he turned, lashing out blindly with his arms. She wasn't there. The corridor was full of dust and dirt, but the ghost had gone.

He realised his hands were empty. He had dropped the gun. He looked down, saw it, bent to reach it, and half fell after a sudden spasm of pain from his leg, but when he straightened he had the gun in his hand.

The ghost had gone. Could she have got past him and run back into the Tower? No.

Steadying himself with one hand on the wall, he moved towards the airlock. His vision began to clear. The explosion had been small, its effect magnified by the close confines of the corridor. It had been very small, he realised. All it had done was blow a neat hole through the central locking mechanism. The doors had been pushed apart.

Ely limped into the airlock.

A message came up on his wristboard. 'I can't see you. What happened? Where are you?'

He ignored it.

The outer doors seemed undamaged. As he got closer he saw why. There was no lock on them. Nor, like the other doors in the Tower, did they slide back into the wall. They opened outwards, on hinges.

Bracing himself for the cold and rain and suffocating wind, he pushed the doors open.

Light.

That was the first thing he registered.

It was everywhere.

As his vision slowly adjusted, he saw blue.

Blue sky.

There was no wind, just a gentle breeze.

There was no rain. The air was filled with a dry heat. Automatically, he took a breath. The air was sweet, rich, with a beguilingly unfamiliar fragrance. Gun in hand, and for the first time in his life, he stepped outside.

It was a transport pad. Or it had been, long ago. The roof was flat in one corner, and jutting out over the edge of the building stood a raised area of cracked black asphalt. On it, bafflingly, someone once had painted a letter 'H'. Out of the middle, its purple flowers and wide leaves waving back and forth, grew a spindly eight-foot high shrub.

Something buzzed past his ear. He jerked out of the way. A small, mostly orange insect hovered in the air a few inches from his face. He marvelled at it for a moment until he was distracted by the noise. His ears were still ringing. No, not ringing. There was another sound, a low steady drone. He looked up and saw four large windmills towering above him. Their white paint was chipped and stained with rust. Only three of the turbines were moving.

"Welcome to the real world, Ely. What do you think?" It was the ghost. In his shock, Ely had temporarily forgotten about her.

"The rain..." was all he could find to say.

"It's the summer," she said. "It hasn't rained much for months. But it will. Give it a few weeks and there will be weeks of rain. After that there will be snow, but then the sun will come out again. It always does. It always has."

He turned slowly around. She was leaning against a wide metal vent. He began to raise the gun.

"Don't, Ely," she warned. "Just look around."

"I've seen outside," he said. "Down in the Twilight Room."

"And was there anywhere more aptly named? They're just screens, Ely. It wasn't real. Don't take my word for it. Just look around for yourself."

He did. He looked down at the dry grey roof, at the thriving shrub, at the yellow-flowered weeds growing out of the cracks around the metal vents.

"Who are you?" he asked.

She told him.

Chapter 11 - Death Comes To Us All Election Day

Twenty minutes later Ely walked back through the airlock. He hesitated at the end of the corridor. He didn't think she was lying, but he had to see for himself.

A voice in his head told him there wasn't time. A louder, newer voice said that, now, there wasn't anything but time. He turned left and kept walking, past the infirmary, until he reached the doors of Councillor Cornwall's office.

He'd seen the doors before. Not often. He wasn't meant to patrol Level Seventy-Seven, but on a few occasions when he'd had to visit the nurses, he had gone to look at the doors to the office that he hoped would one day be his.

The doors themselves were identical to all the others in the Tower, save that there was a small plaque affixed to the wall next to them that read, 'Office of the Councillor. Meetings by Appointment Only.'

He'd never been inside. He'd never tried to make an appointment.

There was no panel by the door. Nor was there one of those old fashioned handles he'd seen down in the tunnels. He tried to lever the doors apart. They didn't move. He rapped his knuckles against the metal. They rang with a dull, solid, thump.

He nodded to himself. Now he knew. There was nothing behind the door but a few inches of metal, and then the outside. Ely looked at the door for a moment longer.

His wristboard chimed. It was a message from Vauxhall, 'Where are you Ely?'

He looked up at the camera in the ceiling of the corridor. Slowly, he took his wristboard off and laid it on the floor.

He ignored the elevators, made his way back to the access ladder, and began to climb down.

Each time he reached the bottom of a ladder and had to go out into the corridor to find another hatch, he found the hallways full of workers. A few, not many, still patiently queued. Others, and again, not many, looked as if they were trying to record and upload the event. Most were talking heatedly to one another, tapping out messages or throwing angry questions up at the cameras. When they saw him, some approached. When they saw his expression, they backed away.

He paused briefly at Level Three. The doors to the Control Room were open. He went inside. The room was empty. The screens were blank. He had been expecting that. It didn't matter. He knew where he was going. He made his way back down to The Foundations.

The flashlight he'd taken from near the ghost's body was where he'd left it, next to the panel leaning up against the Tower wall. He took it and climbed down the ladder.

At the bottom he didn't head towards the hall where he had fought the ghost. He turned the other way. Using the light, he followed the corridor. The passageway appeared blocked after twenty yards. He played the light up and down until he found the old metal filing cabinet. He pushed it out of the way, revealing a narrow opening just wide enough for a person to squeeze through.

Beyond, the corridor was far cleaner, covered in the same white panels he knew from the Tower above. He counted out the distance as he walked. After two hundred yards he stopped and examined the wall. He found the hidden door. He opened it. Inside was a stairwell. He shone the light down. Five steps below, water lapped against the stairs. He went up.

After two flights, the stairs ended in a short landing, with another door. He opened it.

He stepped outside. This time, there was no moment of blinding light.

It was the smell that struck him first. From the roof it had seemed almost fragrant. Here at ground level, it was far richer, with a darker, earthier tone. It was so intoxicating it filled his sense, yet it was forgotten a moment later when he heard the sounds. There were so many, and they were so alien it took him a few seconds to realise they weren't all one sound, but many hundreds of smaller ones. Birds, he thought, birds and insects, chirruping and singing and calling to one another. They sounded nothing like those pale imitations he'd heard on the old movies.

But the street did look almost familiar. He'd seen it before, somewhere, sometime, perhaps in a photograph, though in that memory it looked achingly different to what he saw now.

The street, stretching off for a mile in either direction, was at least forty feet wide, bracketed on either side by the ruins of once tall buildings. The roadway was broken with grass and weeds that had spread up and over piles of rubble. He looked to his left and saw a tree growing up out of the concrete. Its branches had pushed through the windows of a nearby building. As the tree had grown, the branches had ripped up through the brickwork, causing the facade to fracture and break. The fallen masonry now lay in a jumbled heap at the tree's base.

Beyond the tree lay other mounds of broken masonry and twisted metal, all covered in the same irregular sea of green leaves and flowering colours. It was the second most beautiful thing Ely had ever seen.

"Who are you?" he had asked the ghost.

"I was like you," she said. "Or I was a worker, anyway. Up until four years ago I worked down in the Assembly."

"I don't recognise you."

"How many workers would you recognise?" she had retorted. "We were recruited, the three of us, to go out and see what had become of the world. We weren't the first. But we were determined that we would be the last."

"What does that mean?" he had asked.

"Go to the edge of the roof and look down. You'll see for yourself."

Warily, still expecting some kind of trap, he had inched his way over to the side of the building and peered over the edge. It was both the most terrible, and the most beautiful, sight he had ever seen.

"There's no water. No flood," he had said. Below him were the ruins of buildings, stretching off as far as the eye could see.

"The city, the real city, was built long ago by a river. It does flood, occasionally, but after a few days, the water level drops, and the streets clear again."

"They said it was built in the most remote part of the country. They said, before the rains began, before the flood, that there was a great toxic desert outside."

"I think," she said, *"that was partly true. It was never a desert, it was always like this, but it was toxic. There was some Great Disaster, though I doubt it happened quite as they told us. People did die, and they died suddenly. We found their remains in buildings and houses across the city and far beyond. We don't know what killed them, not exactly, but we suspect it was done by the same people who originally built the Tower."*

Ely turned and looked up at the Tower that had been his home, his life. It wasn't the gleaming edifice depicted in the pictures. The solar panels still covered the walls, but they appeared dented, some were cracked, others were clearly damaged beyond use.

"If there was no flood," he'd said, looking down at the ruined city below, *"then there's no tidal barrier. Where does the Tower get its power from?"*

"Solar panels. Body heat. The turbines." She pointed at the giant wind turbines towering over them. *"And the machines in that Recreation Room, of course."*

"They said the solar panels were replaced with panelling that captured the kinetic energy of the wind and rain."

"They said a lot of things, Ely."

"And I should believe you, and not them?"

"You should believe the evidence of your own eyes."

He looked up and down, and around.

"How long?" he asked. *"I mean, if there was no Great Disaster, then has it really been sixty years?"*

"No," she said, *"it's been a lot longer than that. The Tower was built as an enclosed system. It was a marvel for its time, designed to be a net producer of energy and heat. Those who constructed it utilised the most advanced technologies of their age. And those technologies were developed to take our species to Mars, that much is true. But turbines break."* She gestured to the idle windmill. *"The self-cleaning system for the solar panels clog, and the panels become obscured by dirt. It was meant to last one hundred years. Exactly how much longer or shorter than that it's been, we can't be sure, but the technology is finally failing."*

"Thanks to your sabotage."

"No, it was falling apart long before we returned. It was like this long before we left. It was why the microphones were turned off, why most of the servers are silent, there isn't the energy to keep them going. That was why the Recreation Room was created. It is why the population keeps getting smaller."

Ely looked along the road at the broken buildings. The city was a ruin. But it wasn't dead. Birds and insects meant food. A broken building could still offer shelter. A river meant water. There was life. More than that, it was a place in which people could live.

"Some people must have known, they must have learnt the truth."

"Of course. Or they realised that something didn't add up. And they would talk to one another, and they would ask questions. But that's sedition, isn't it, Ely? And what happens to people who demonstrate seditious behaviour?"

"They're sent to Tower-Thirteen," he replied automatically.

"Look around. Look behind you. Look at the skyline. There are no other Towers. There is no launch site. There are no transports. Look down, Ely, that is the city."

"What happened to them? All those people, the people I sentenced."

"I told you. It's an enclosed system. Energy. Water. Food. You can only get out what you put in."

"I didn't know..." he began.

"No, you didn't. And you didn't even suspect. They chose you a long time ago, Ely. They trained you for this. They bred you for it. You had no friends growing up, no attachments, no family, nothing but the Tower and the City and your belief in it. They needed you, or someone like you, because they knew that the time was coming when people would have to leave the Tower."

"Who? Who chose me?"

"You know the answer to that," she replied.

"Hello, Ely," Arthur said.

Ely slowed turned around. Arthur stood in the shadow of a doorway thirty yards up the road.

"There's no Chancellor," Ely said. "No Councillors."

"No," Arthur said.

"There's just you?"

"More or less." The old man spoke with a casual lack of concern.

"The colony ships, the elections, none of it was real?"

"Not quite," Arthur said. "The elections were real enough. Everyone voted and every vote was counted."

"But the candidates were fake?" Ely took a step away from the Tower. Arthur stayed in the shadows of the doorway.

"I tried having a real candidate, once. It didn't work. Some people don't know how to follow orders."

"And the newsfeeds, were those fabricated too?"

"Some. Some. Just enough to keep the debate heading in the right direction. But most of it was the same rehashed rumours repeated day in day out, created by a populace eager to have the same olds in their news. It was ever thus."

"Is that a joke?" Ely asked.

"I'm just trying to lighten the mood," Arthur said. He was grinning Ely saw, but there was only a dark menace to the older man's expression.

Ely looked away, turning his gaze to the building opposite the Tower. It was vast, stretching perhaps a quarter of a mile. The ruins were dwarfed by the Tower, but somehow that made the older building seem more impressive. Through the broken windows, Ely could see that the roof had collapsed. Inside, taking advantage of the sunlight and shelter, grew a forest of those same purple flowering shrubs that he'd seen on the Tower's roof. Ely took a few steps out into the street, towards it.

"Well, boy, don't you have anything you want to say? Anything you want to ask?" Arthur called out.

Ely took another step towards the building. With a cacophonous flapping of wings, a score of small red-breasted birds erupted out through the broken windows.

Ely turned and watched as they circled up the street, coming to land on the roof of a building further up the street.

"I said, don't you have anything you want to ask?" Arthur called out, this time with irritated impatience.

"Are they robins?" Ely asked.

"What?" Arthur replied.

"Those birds, are they robins?" Ely asked again. He glanced back down the street towards Arthur. He took another step, and the old man was out of sight.

"Those? No," Arthur said, stepping out of the shadow of the doorway. "They're starlings, I think."

"The woman. The ghost. Robin, that's her name."

"Her name is Oxford," Arthur said. "Considering the location, I'd say that's almost poetic."

"She changed it. They all did. Her name's Robin. The man who killed Gower and Bradford, his name was Gabriel. The woman who died in the elevator shaft, she was called Fern."

Arthur snorted with derision.

"So you spoke to her, then?" he asked.

"A little."

"Where is she?"

"Dead. She fell off the roof. Her body should be around here somewhere."

"I see."

There was a moment's silence. Ely turned to look up at the Tower once more.

"Why did you do it?" Ely asked.

"Why? What do you mean, 'why'? Look about you, do you actually think people can live out here, in *this*?"

"I think they can try."

"And they'd die. That's what would happen. So you spoke to your ghost. Did she tell you what she was meant to do? Her and the other two? They were meant to go out into this wasteland and find out whether our species could survive. Is the water toxic? Is there food we can eat? Those were the questions she was meant to answer. She didn't though. We thought we saw them die. We were convinced of it. Very clever on her part, that was. Far cleverer than I thought she was capable of. But it was a betrayal of everyone in the Tower. A betrayal of her species."

154

"You think she betrayed you?"

"Like I said, she was meant to tell us whether we could survive out here. Without that knowledge, we had to stay inside, where we could live, where we could survive."

"We weren't the first to be chosen to go out," she said. *"I don't know how many went out before us and I don't know what happened to them. They sent us out to see what the world was like. And we did. And when we returned and we told them it was a place of wondrous abundance, they tried to kill us. They thought they had succeeded. But we didn't die, because from that first moment we looked up and saw the stars, we knew what fate awaited us if we weren't prepared."*

Ely gestured over his shoulder at the Tower. He didn't look at it.

"The City of Britain. Was the name a joke too?"

"That's what the place was called before I was born. I think that was what the people who built the Tower wanted it to become."

"And you were born in the Tower," Ely stated.

"I was," Arthur answered.

"You didn't know the world before." Again it was a statement, but again the old man took it as a question.

"No, but it wasn't always like this, Ely. The air was polluted. It was toxic. You couldn't spend more than a few minutes outside without getting sick. When I was young, younger than you, there was a clock outside what's now the Assemblies. It was counting down one hundred years. That was how long we had to wait. When I took power, I got rid of the clock. I had to. There are some things we need to remember, but many more that we need to forget."

"So you destroyed the archives. All the old movies and books. There were millions of them, once."

"She told you that, did she? It's an exaggeration. There were a few thousand, no more than that. And yes, I erased a lot of them, but they were useless. They took up valuable storage space whilst giving people nothing but the wrong kind of ideas. I understood, you see, when no one else did. People couldn't know the sacrifice they were making, not fully.

For that part that they were aware of, they needed a reason. They needed an idea, one that could be turned and twisted into something useful when the time was right. I gave them a goal, a grand idea. They had the dream of achieving something their ancestors had failed at. Mars."

"It was that easy?"

"Easy? You think it was easy? I've worked everyday for the betterment of my species. I've given up my life to ensure that humanity will continue stronger, purer, able to reconquer the world. It was never easy."

"And now it's over," Ely said. "The Tower has failed. People will have to leave."

"The explosions have brought that time forwards," Arthur said. "But that time was coming, anyway. Yes, people will have to leave, and they will need to be led."

"By you?"

"No, no. Not by me," Arthur snapped. "Weren't you listening, boy? If I'd just wanted power I could have had it long ago. This is about our species, about our future. No, I won't lead. I'll be the villain, the puppet-master who kept you all imprisoned these decades past. I will become the devil future generations will fear and revile. But I won't care, because my job has been done."

"Who then? Or are you expecting me to be their leader?"

"You? No, you're a brawler. You're good in a fight, but you're not a thinker."

"Then who?" he asked, again.

"Me, Ely." Vauxhall stepped out from a doorway about twenty feet down the street from Arthur. Like the older man, she kept one of her hands behind her back.

"Hello Vox. I thought you'd be around here somewhere. So, why did you do it?" Ely asked.

"I found out twenty years ago. I was only ten, and I worked out how to hack into the system. I found out, and Arthur found me. He offered me a job. He taught me everything and then, together, we came up with the plan. It was the only way, Ely. The Tower was failing. More energy was being consumed than generated. We did our best to keep things going, but we knew it wouldn't be long before we had to venture out into this wasteland. We had to prepare. We had to prepare the people. More than that, we had to ensure we had the right people. It took us a generation, but we're nearly ready. Most of the people in the Tower are of the right sort, the right mentality. There are just a few more to weed out."

"You mean those forty-seven suspects. You were the one who left that note for Penrith?"

"It wasn't her, it was me," Arthur said.

"Which amounts to the same thing," Ely said. "You planted the note as a test, to see who was loyal and who wasn't?"

"The woman, Penrith, she told over four hundred people over the course of a year," Vauxhall said. "Only forty-six of them proved unreliable. The others all reported it."

"But not to me," Ely said.

"Oh, some did," Vauxhall said. "I intercepted their messages. I didn't want you finding out before it was time. I won't apologise for it, Ely. It was a necessary deception. There's a time coming when we need to know upon whom we can rely."

"I don't imagine for a moment that you're going to apologise for anything that you've done," Ely said. "But when I asked you why you'd done it, I was talking about the murders."

"We didn't kill Gower or Bradford," Arthur said. "That was your ghost."

"Gabriel, yes. I know. You needed those two nurses. Who else was there to deal with people supposedly sent for transport to Tower-Thirteen? They were killers, real murderers."

"That wasn't murder," Arthur said. "The Tower was failing. It grew inefficient. More energy was being consumed than created. The population had to be pruned. And who else should I have sacrificed, if not the subversives whose deviance imperilled the future of our species. It wasn't murder. It was housekeeping."

"It was murder. The deaths of Gower and Bradford weren't. That was revenge. But I'm not talking about those deaths." Ely gauged the distance between himself, Vauxhall and Arthur. He began to walk slowly up the street towards them.

"No," he said, turning to look at Vauxhall once more, "I want to know why you murdered the Greenes."

She said nothing.

"I knew something was wrong with the wounds. Something was wrong with the timing too. You tried to throw me off track. Both of you. You did a good job. I was concentrating so much on whether the crime took place at three a.m. that I forgot to consider how someone could sleep through the pod being opened and their spouse being murdered right next to them. Of course, I was tired. I suppose that's why you picked that time for the murder, but," he took another step forwards, "I might have worked it out earlier if you hadn't destroyed most of the archives. If Gabriel hadn't killed Gower and Bradford, if he'd not slit their throats in revenge, if the blood hadn't sprayed out onto the walls, I may never have realised. But he did. And I did. Eventually."

"I didn't slit their throats," Vauxhall said.

"No," he agreed, "you didn't. It was Arthur or Gower or Bradford. It doesn't matter which, because they didn't kill the Greenes. Their hearts had stopped beating long before the blade sliced through their throats. What was it you said? You control the pods and the air-filtration system? You just cut off their air supply. Tell me why."

"When we came back," the ghost said, "we told them what we found. And they tried to kill us. They thought they had succeeded. But we couldn't leave. The woman who died in that elevator shaft, Fern, she was Finnya Greene's sister. She wouldn't leave her family here. She wanted to help them escape. We had to stay close, but we couldn't risk hiding outside. We hid in the only place we knew they wouldn't look. The tunnels. You see, we discovered what they really were, how this city is honeycombed with them. We got access to The Foundations, and to the servers. We found out how to hack into the system and we learnt to watch them, and we watched you. It took us years before we discovered how to alter the records and camera footage and then we had to find

clothes, and then, oh and then... It took so long. But we finally managed to make contact with Finnya."

"That was six months ago?" Ely asked.

"Yes, how did you know?"

"That was when she handed back her visor," he said.

"Ah," she nodded. "It wasn't easy. And it wasn't easy persuading her of the truth. Nor was it easy for her to persuade her family to come with us. But it was all in place. We were going to spirit them out, and at the same time we would cripple the Tower. Everyone would discover the truth and then do with that whatever they wished. We would be long gone. We were going to act today. It was always today, the day of the election. It seemed fitting."

"We suspected she knew something," Vauxhall said. "Handing back that visor, not communicating on-net, and then there was the night the camera moved in her room. She was up to something, and we couldn't allow that."

"So you wanted me to think it was Penrith? She didn't recognise the clothing. I just assumed she was lying. But she wasn't, was she? She had nothing to do with the deaths. She didn't know Fern or the Greenes. You planted that evidence, because you wanted me to execute someone."

"She was guilty, Ely. It was a test to see whether you were up to what comes next. Whether you would be prepared to help lead your people out into this Promised Land."

"And it was you who shot at me. Or one of you. I suppose you needed me to think the threat was real. You know, it's almost funny," Ely said, as he walked around a mound that appeared to be more metal than moss. "You must have spent a long time working out which room could be accessed without someone appearing on the cameras. But then it turned out that the ghosts actually could get into the system and wipe the records. All that effort on your part, all wasted. But because of it, because they died, all the rest of these events occurred. The woman who died in that elevator, her name was Fern, and she was Finnya Greene's sister. All she wanted to do was get her family out of the Tower. The killing of Gower and Bradford aside, they don't believe in killing. Even after you had murdered her sister, Fern didn't come after you. She wanted to lead me up to the roof. Fern wanted me to see the truth. She thought that she controlled the elevator. But you still had control of that, Vox. You disconnected the brakes. You caused it to plummet. That's another death on your hands."

"Oh, enough," Arthur snapped. "If you want to count them like that, then there are thousands of deaths on each of our hands. But the scales are balanced by the lives we've saved."

"After Fern's death, I told Gabriel that we shouldn't kill. That we shouldn't become like them. I thought he'd taken it to heart. We went back to our original plan. We'd set off the charges, and rescue the children. Gabriel and I went to plant the bombs. On the way back he saw those nurses. *I couldn't stop him. And then he died in that stupid accident. Do you think his death was justice? Do you think it was just?"*

"I don't know," Ely said.

"Twelve thousand people, Ely, the future of our species. Individuals don't matter, they can't." Arthur said.

"Is it just twelve thousand?" Ely asked. "Are there no others?"

"It's just us," Vauxhall said. "The Tower, the City of Britain."

"It was a great nation once," Arthur said, pointing at the buildings. "I've read the books, it controlled the world. From its ruins an even greater nation will arise. With your help."

"Where were you going to take the children?" Ely asked.

"We found a farm. It had been abandoned a few seasons before. Crops had grown wild in the fields, but they were there. The buildings were empty, but people had lived in them, and recently. We thought that perhaps we could find them."

"Now, are you finished with the questions?" Arthur asked. "Because we do have work to do. We need to see if the Tower can be repaired. If it can't, then we need to act quickly to maintain control of the situation."

"I've one last question," Ely said.

"What?" Arthur snapped impatiently.

"If there are no ships being built, then what is it that everyone's doing in the Assemblies?"

"Keeping busy. Keeping occupied. Staying useful," Arthur said. "That's all anyone ever wants out of life, isn't it? To be safe, to be comfortable and to have a purpose."

"I see."

Ely glanced between Vauxhall and Arthur. Then he looked up. A solitary bird flew out of the window above him. It circled overhead once before coming to settle on a twisted lamppost.

"So, unless there's anything else, it's time to make your choice," Arthur said. "I told you that time was coming. I gave you that gun. I see you've still got it. So join us, or shoot us now. It is time for you to choose."

Ely took another step. He was thirty yards away from the door to the tunnel. Arthur was closest, at around twenty yards away. Vauxhall stood ten feet behind and a dozen feet to the right of the old man. Both, he noted, still had their hands behind their backs.

Slowly he moved his hand to the pistol at his waist. As he did, he saw both Arthur and Vauxhall visibly relax. He took the gun out, then tossed it through a broken window.

Arthur looked surprised. Vauxhall looked relieved.

"What now?" Ely asked, he took another step forwards. "I mean, if you want Vauxhall to lead the people, what happens to you?"

"Like I said, the Tower was my life. I'll stay, once everyone else has left."

Ely stopped, suddenly, and stared at the ground.

"What's that?" he wondered out loud, as he bent down.

"It's a beguiling story," Ely said, raising the pistol again, "and I can see that some of it's true. But how much? You've no proof that Fern was Finnya Greene's sister. And if there ever was any, it's now been destroyed."

"Proof? You want proof? You want more proof than that what you can see. If you pull that trigger, you will die. That's not a threat. It's a fact. The gun's rigged. Where do you think we learnt about explosives? Out in the wild? We were taught by that old

man. There's a button on the side. If you press it, the magazine will come out. At least if it was real gun with proper ammunition in it, it would."

Ely looked down at the pistol.

"Try it. It's not a trick." She raised her hands, and this time Ely saw they were empty.

He pressed the button. The magazine fell, but only by half an inch. Carefully, he pulled it out. There were no cartridges, just something wrapped in silver coloured plastic. There were two wires leading from the plastic into the body of the pistol.

"They've tried that before," she said.

"Why me?" he asked. "Why are you telling me? Why did you want me to follow you?"

"I told you, we only came back because of Finnya's family. I'm going to honour her wishes and take the children somewhere safe. As for you, for at least the last five years you are culpable in all the deaths this Tower has caused. But you were an unwitting accomplice, Ely, a prisoner like all the others. We decided we would give you back your life, we were curious to see what you would do with it."

"And what about me?" Ely asked, still kneeling.

"The workers will think you're leading them," Vauxhall said. "You just won an election. You fought the killers that had been terrorising the Tower, and in doing so you discovered the truth. You'll lead them out here."

"And then where?" he reached down to his boot, and palmed the spring powered bolt gun.

"And that's why you'll be the leader in name only," Vauxhall continued. "I've found a spot, somewhere not far. There are buildings there that we can use. I'd hoped that—"

In one smooth motion, Ely stood and raised his arm, pointing the bolt gun at Arthur. He pulled the trigger. The bolt flew out with barely a sound. The old man collapsed.

Ely turned.

Vauxhall's arm came up, a pistol in her hand. She fired. Ely was hit. As the force of the impact spun him around his finger tightened on the trigger. The bolt flew.

Expecting another shot, he turned his head. If he was going to die, he wanted the last thing he saw to be the sky. There was no second shot. He looked down the street. Vauxhall was down, but not dead. The bolt had hit her in the thigh. The pistol lay on the ground three feet from her, and she was crawling towards it.

Ely staggered over to her, bent, and picked up the gun. She didn't seem to notice him for a moment. He found the catch, and ejected the magazine. He nodded.

"Ely, please, you can't."

"You killed them in their sleep," he said. "Not just the Greenes, but everyone. They always died in their sleep. I suppose it was Arthur who changed the archives, made it look as if that was how people had always died. I thought that was normal. Why would I think any differently?"

Ely replaced the magazine.

"Please. Don't. It would be murder," Vauxhall pleaded.

"No, it wouldn't. Didn't you hear what the Chancellor said? The sentence for the killer was death."

Ely pulled the trigger, twice.

He glanced over at Arthur. The bolt had lodged in the man's chest. He was dead.

The gun was heavy in his hand. He wanted to drop it, but he knew that he would need it in the days to come. He glanced at his shoulder. He had no idea how severe the wound was, nor what he could do about it. He limped a short way from the bodies, to a slightly larger grass covered mound. He sat down.

Time passed.

"I've a bandage if you want one."

It was Robin. She stood in the doorway to the Tower, two children behind her.

"It's over," Ely said.

"Yes, it is." She walked out of the shadows. The two children followed. They weren't the Greenes. Another pair came out, and another. And then he saw Simon and Beatrice Greene.

"You're taking all the children?" he asked.

"Who else will care for them?" she replied.

Ely nodded.

"Here." She knelt beside him, took out a bandage and wrapped it around his shoulder.

"It's not really more than a graze. Your arm doesn't seem to be broken," she said. "But then again, it might be. Keep the wound clean. Maybe you'll live. Maybe you'll die anyway. Death comes to us all, it's how you live that counts."

She stood up and beckoned for the children to follow her. There was quite a crowd of them now. Ely thought he could see some taller figures lurking in the shadows just inside the door.

"We're heading south," she said. "Follow us or don't. It's your choice, Ely."

Robin led the children away, leaving Ely alone. He sat for a while, just listening as terrified youthful murmurs turned to excited chatter which then faded into the distance.

He glanced down the road, then up at the Tower. He had a choice. He had to decide what to do next. But it wasn't really any choice at all. He was the Constable. He had to keep the people safe.

The End.

Printed in Great Britain
by Amazon.co.uk, Ltd.,
Marston Gate.